NOWHERE LIKE HOME

Beth Clarke and her younger sister Lexi have moved to the seaside town of Furze Point, where Beth is set to take over the running of The Beach Hut shop from Tom and Carol Bennett. The town welcomes them, but Lexi is unhappy, and Beth worries that she's made a mistake. Then she meets the enigmatic Noah Walsh, who has returned to Furze Point after a twenty-year absence. But not everyone is pleased to see him . . .

TERESA ASHBY

◆

NOWHERE LIKE HOME

Complete and Unabridged

LINFORD
Leicester

First published in Great Britain in 2021

First Linford Edition
published 2022

A catalogue record for this book is available
from the British Library.

ISBN 978–1–4448–4828–1

Published by
Ulverscroft Limited
Anstey, Leicestershire

Printed and bound in Great Britain by
TJ Books Ltd., Padstow, Cornwall

This book is printed on acid-free paper

A Moment of Panic

Carol woke with a start from a troubled dream and stared up at the ceiling, her hand against her chest. She could feel her heart pounding and it shook her whole body.

Beside her, Tom stirred.

'Is it time to get up?' he murmured sleepily.

'Almost,' she said. Her throat was dry. She had a feeling she'd been whimpering in her sleep.

'Are you OK, Carol?' He turned to look at her. 'You sound a bit strange.'

'I'm fine.' She didn't want to worry him, especially on the day they were shutting the door on their past.

'I'll put the kettle on.'

Tom threw back the duvet and got up. Moments later, she could hear him clinking mugs and boiling the kettle. They were such reassuring sounds.

'It was just a dream,' she whispered to herself as she sat up to turn off the alarm. 'Just a dream. It wasn't real.'

The nightmare was triggered by her credit card being declined yesterday. She'd only been to the florist to buy flowers for Beth, who was taking over at the Beach Hut today. The Beach Hut had been their home and livelihood since they were newlyweds and it felt strange to be handing it over to someone else now they'd retired.

It had left her feeling curiously adrift and she knew Tom was feeling it, too.

Her thoughts went back to the florist yesterday and her insides squirmed with embarrassment and fear.

'I'm so sorry, Carol,' Jilly had said. 'Your card has been declined. There must be a glitch in the system. Do you want to try it again?'

'Of course,' Carol said, but the card was declined again.

'Have you a different card?'

'My debit card,' she said, rummaging through her purse, but that was declined, too. 'I'll pay cash.'

Her hand shook as she slotted the

cards back in her purse, but there wasn't enough money in there to pay for the flowers. Not even close.

She could hardly bear to meet Jilly's sympathetic eyes.

'I'm sorry. I'll leave them for now,' she'd said, aware of pitying looks from others in the shop.

'You can pay me later, Carol. I trust you.'

'No!' she'd said. 'No, I can't do that. I'm sorry. The flowers were a silly idea anyway. Beth might be allergic or something.'

'Are you all right, Carol?' Jilly looked genuinely concerned. 'It's really nothing to worry about. It happens all the time.'

'Not to me, it doesn't,' Carol muttered as she escaped from the shop. She shuddered now remembering how sharp she was with poor Jilly, as if it was her fault.

To make matters worse, she'd gone to the cash machine on the way home, but it said she had insufficient funds. What on earth was that supposed to mean?

She was in quite a state by the time

3

she got home, convinced they'd been the victims of some sort of fraud.

'Now stop worrying,' Tom said calmly. 'I'll sort it all out. As for the credit card, you know what they're like. It'll be a glitch in the system.'

He shut himself in the kitchen and he was ages talking on the phone, but when he came out, he was smiling.

'All sorted. Don't worry, it was just a mistake. These things happen.'

'I hope you said how embarrassing it was,' she said. 'There were other people in the shop. They were all looking at me.'

'Forget about it, Carol,' he said. 'I've managed to arrange a small overdraft to tide us over until our final wages go in and the credit card company has agreed to raise our credit limit.'

'Are things really tight for us, Tom?'

'We just have to be careful, that's all,' he said. 'I didn't realise quite how much work this place needed, but we'll get straight again.'

She nodded. When they'd lived at the Beach Hut, the council had taken care of any repairs and renovations. It wasn't until they'd bought and moved into the bungalow that they realised it needed a new central heating system.

That was on top of the work they already knew needed to be done.

'I can't believe we've come to this. In our sixties and running up a huge credit card bill, not to mention the mortgage. It's not as if we're extravagant and as from now, we lose our income from the Beach Hut.'

Somehow they'd ended up with no spare cash for the unexpected and it seemed that one unexpected thing after another had happened lately.

'We've just hit a bad patch, that's all. We'll soon be back on an even keel.'

It brought back worries from her childhood when her dad used to hide from the debt collectors.

He'd brought her up on his own after her mum passed away and he struggled to work and take care of his daughter. He was such a sweet, loving man who wanted Carol to have the best of everything, but

5

it had come at such a cost.

He wasn't reckless with money, far from it; they simply didn't have enough.

Tom reminded her of her father in many ways and she smiled when he came in with a mug of tea and put it down on her bedside table.

'Are you sure you're all right, Carol? You look pale.'

'I've got a bit of a headache.'

'Not still fretting about the finances, are you?'

'No, of course not,' she fibbed. 'I had a bit of a nightmare and it's left me feeling unsettled.'

'Drink your tea and I'll get you some pills for your head,' he said. 'Then how do you fancy breakfast in bed? You can have a lie in and hopefully shake the headache off.'

'That sounds lovely, Tom,' she said, 'but I ought to come with you to welcome Beth.'

'You'll have lots of chances to do that. I'll head up to the Beach Hut in a bit and get ready for the handover while you get yourself ready for our afternoon tea at the Lighthouse.'

'I'd forgotten about that,' she said.

'Forgotten? But you've been looking forward to it for ages.'

'I know,' she said. Her mind had been on other things for quite a while. 'Perhaps we should cancel it.'

'That wouldn't be fair on Rosita, would it?' Tom said. 'She'll have got stuff in for us specially. Try not to worry about money, love. Something will come up. It always does.'

Her dad used to say that.

The looks people had given her yesterday reminded her of the day the television rental company came to take their television away when she was a child.

'Please, don't do this,' her dad had said, following the men out to their van. 'I'm only a couple of months behind. I'll make it up.'

A couple of the neighbours were in the street, watching as he turned round and gathered Carol up in his arms.

'I'm so sorry, sweetheart,' he said.

'I've messed up again, but don't worry. Something will come up.'

Later that day, one of their neighbours had knocked on the door. Something did indeed come up.

'No offence, but we wondered if you'd like our old telly? We've just got a new one. We don't want anything for it and it's not great, but it'll tide you over until you can sort out another.'

Her dad was crying when he came back in. Kindness did that to people.

But she couldn't rely on anyone else getting them out of this mess. But right now she had to forget all that and start looking forward to their afternoon tea.

* * *

As the town came into view, Noah took his foot off the accelerator, slowing down so he could drink it all in.

It was exactly as he remembered it, even though he hadn't been back since he was a child. The feeling hadn't changed. It didn't matter whether the town was swathed in fog, made grey by rain, or as it was today, bathed in sunshine, the sight of it warmed his soul.

In his memory this was a place of sand and sunshine and the feeling of being contented and safe. Never in his life had he felt like that anywhere but here.

But as he drew closer, he felt a hard knot form in his stomach as the warm feelings deserted him. This was unexpected. He thought it would feel like coming home after the happy times he'd spent here, but an almost savage resentment filled his heart.

He was unprepared for the fury that welled up inside. He'd thought all that was well and truly in the past, but as he looked down at the town so precious in his memory, he felt overwhelmed with anger at what he'd lost, what had been taken from him.

He pulled into a parking area at the front of a large black barn with a painted sign, *Bluebell Farm Shop*. He stopped for a moment, breathing hard, trying to make sense of his tumultuous thoughts.

A woman came out of the shop followed by a man carrying a box full of produce which he carefully placed in her car boot. He'd know that red-haired giant anywhere. Fergus! He looked just like his father, but the farm had changed beyond recognition.

Fergus looked over at Noah and frowned and he felt a moment of panic. If Fergus recognised him, there'd be no going back. He turned the car round and headed away from Furze Point, back to civilisation which he should never have left in the first place.

He was wrong to come back here and it was a mistake he didn't intent to repeat.

10

A Knight of the Road

'This can't be it,' Lexi said as she clung to her seat. 'You must have taken a wrong turning. Isn't it dangerous to drive down roads like this, Beth? There's no way this is a main road. I think you should turn around.'

It was the most she'd said for the past four hours. Beth welcomed the fact that her sister was at least speaking to her now, but wished it wasn't to be so negative.

'It's fine,' Beth said calmly. 'I've driven here before and I'm driving carefully, I promise, and yes, I'm afraid it is the main and only road into Furze Point.'

On either side of the road were rolling fields surrounded with gorse bushes.

'See those bushes?' Beth said. 'It's gorse, otherwise known as furze. When I came here earlier in the year, it was smothered in bright yellow flowers.'

Lexi sighed. She couldn't be less interested.

The views were lovely, but the road was narrow and full of twists and turns.

The car was so loaded with stuff that Beth couldn't see through her rear view mirror, but had to rely on her wing mirrors.

'I still don't understand why we have to move all the way out here,' Lexi grumbled, folding her arms and slouching down in her seat. 'We should turn around and go home now before it's too late.'

Beth was tired of explaining. She pulled in to a passing space to let a car go by in the opposite direction and there was an ominous bump as the car leaned to one side. The other driver waved a friendly thank you as he passed by.

'That's why,' Beth said. 'It's a different way of life out here. People are friendly. They care. There's no mad rush here.'

'Life? Is that what you call it?'

'I know you're cross, love, but I'm doing this for us,' Beth said.

'You can count me out,' Lexi said. 'I will never call this place home. Ever.

And I probably won't come here in the holidays if I have to endure this nightmare drive. Aren't there any trains? And what was that bump?'

Beth tried not to be stung by her sister's words. She'd hoped she'd come round and perhaps she would once she saw their new home. It was still early days, after all.

'You can get a train to Stoursley and then I could pick you up by boat and bring you back to Furze Point,' Beth said hopefully.

'You don't know anything about boats,' Lexi pointed out.

'I'm going to have to learn. We're almost there, Lexi. Keep watching. I promise, you're going to love it.' She made to pull out of the passing space, but her wheels spun.

'What is it?' Lexi cried out in alarm. 'What's happened?'

'I pulled too far over,' Beth said. She had to stay calm. Panicking and accelerating would only bury them deeper in the mud. 'That must have been what the bump was. There's a dip at the edge.'

'Oh, great,' Lexi muttered, rolling her eyes. 'I suppose we have to sit here for hours now waiting to be rescued.'

'Not at all,' Beth said cheerfully. 'Come on, out you get. There must be a way of getting ourselves out of this. I can probably use the car mats for traction.'

Groaning, Lexi hauled herself out of the car.

'Ew, Beth,' she called out, 'I'm covered in mud now.'

Beth felt a nervous laugh bubbling up inside, but she mustn't let it out. If Lexi thought she was laughing at her, it could be the last straw.

'It'll wash off,' she said.

'That's supposed to make me feel better? Look at the state of my trainers. And I don't see how a couple of car mats are going to get you out of that mess. Do you?'

Beth had buried the nearside wheels deep in the mud. She had no idea there was such a drop off at the edge of the passing space and knew she'd have to be more careful in future, but Lexi was right. Car mats probably wouldn't cut it.

'You're going to need a shovel,' Lexi said. 'Have you got one?'

'Not on me, no,' Beth said shortly. She only carried a shovel in winter when snow was forecast. Somehow she'd never envisaged herself getting stuck in mud. She looked round just as Lexi stepped out in the road and waved her arms in the air.

'Lexi, wait! What are you doing?'

A car coming from Furze Point stopped abruptly, the window opened and an angry face glared out at them.

'Are you trying to get yourself killed?'

'This is why you moved here, remember?' Lexi said over her shoulder. 'Everyone being so friendly and helpful.'

'I'm so sorry,' Beth stepped forward. 'My sister was just trying to flag you down because she thought we needed help. My car is stuck in the mud, but don't worry, I can sort it out.'

She expected him to put his foot down and drive off, but now he was over the shock of having Lexi leap out in front of him, his face softened into a smile, and what a smile it was.

Perhaps it was just the sight of a friendly face after hours in the car with Lexi glaring at her.

'You're going to need a tow,' he said. 'Hold on. I'll turn round further along and come back. I've got a tow rope in the boot. We'll have you back on the road in no time.'

'Thank you,' Beth said.

'Don't thank me until I've got you out,' he said with a grin.

His car was a big beast and Beth had no doubt it would have the power to pull them out of their predicament.

'Did you see his eyes, Lexi?' Beth said as they waited for him to come back. 'Have you ever seen eyes so blue? They're like a twilight winter sky.'

Lexi laughed.

'Twilight winter sky?' she scoffed. 'No, I didn't notice, to be honest. I was checking out if his car looked hefty enough to get us out of this mess. Don't tell me you fancy him. You've only just set eyes on him.'

'Nothing of the sort,' Beth said, her face burning red.

She felt silly. She wished she hadn't said anything. But he did have the most incredible eyes and she'd felt a connection. She wondered if he'd felt it too.

It was all part of the magic of Furze Point. She'd felt as if she belonged here from the very first visit.

'He's not coming back,' Lexi said at the very moment he reappeared and pulled up in front of Beth's car. Lexi turned the other way and feigned interest in the gorse. A moment later, she let out a yelp of pain.

'Are you all right?'

'It's prickly,' Lexi complained.

'Of course it is. It's gorse,' Beth said.

'Well pardon me for not knowing! I've never even seen this stuff before.'

The guy got out of his car and came to stand beside Beth. He was very tall and looked strong.

'The thorns can be quite painful as I

found out when I tried to pick a bunch for my grandmother when I was a kid,' he said. 'I've got a first aid kit in the car if you need it.'

'I'm all right, thanks,' Lexi said. 'It just made me jump, that's all. I thought something had stung me.'

He got a tow rope and a blanket out of the boot then threw the blanket on the ground and sprawled back on it, looking under Beth's car for something to attach the rope to.

'You're from Furze Point?' Beth asked.

'No,' he said. 'Not really. I got as far as Bluebell Farm then got cold feet.'

'Cold feet?'

'Are you moving to the town?' he asked, ignoring her question.

'How did you guess?'

'Car packed to the roof with all sorts.' He grinned as he jumped to his feet and gathered up the muddy blanket. 'Dead giveaway.'

'All our worldly goods,' Beth said and felt a moment of sadness that they had managed to pack their lives into one

18

small car.

'Jump in and let's see if we can get you back on the road. Put it in gear and just touch the accelerator once we start to move. Keep it slow. You jump in, too,' he added to Lexi who was leaning against his car with her arms folded. She couldn't look any more fed up if she tried.

'Sorry, but I'm not wading through the mud again.'

'Back seat?' he suggested.

'You've seen it. You couldn't fit a sheet of paper in there.'

'Lexi,' Beth said. 'He's trying to help us. Stop being so awkward and just get in the car, please.'

'You could stand outside, but you're likely to get more than just your feet muddy. A lot of mud is going to be thrown about,' he warned. He was being very patient considering he'd seemed in quite a hurry, Beth thought, and Lexi was just doing her best to be difficult. 'Or you could sit in the front of my car.'

'No, thanks,' Lexi said. 'I'll take my chances out here.'

'Don't say I didn't warn you.' He got back in his car and started the engine.

Beth was amazed how quickly her car was free of the mud and back on level ground. She left the engine running and got out.

'That was brilliant,' she said as relief flooded over her. 'Thank you so much.'

'My pleasure,' he said as removed the rope. 'I'm not sure your passenger is too happy about it though.'

Beth turned round and saw Lexi standing behind her, shoulders hunched, hands dangling at her sides, mud dripping from her fingers. It was even in her hair.

'Oh, Lexi.'

'Good luck,' he said before getting back in his car and driving off towards Furze Point.

Beth and Lexi were still standing beside the car when he passed them heading out again, giving them a little toot on the horn and a cheery wave.

He was certainly in a hurry to get away.

'If you laugh . . . ' Lexi said furiously.

'I'm not laughing,' Beth said. 'I'm wondering how to get you in the car without getting mud all over it.'

'Really? All you care about is your car?'

'No, Lexi, all I care about is you, believe it or not. Everything I do is for you, every decision I make. You always come first.

'That guy warned you what would happen if you stood there and you chose to ignore his advice. You got yourself into this mess.'

'No, you did,' Lexi shouted. 'This is all your fault.' She burst into tears, but when Beth tried to comfort her, she squirmed away. 'I'll never forgive you for this, Beth. You've ruined my life.'

'Get in the car, Lexi,' Beth said wearily. 'Let's get you home so you can have a shower. I'll clean the car up later.'

'Home?' Lexi stopped crying and the hopeful look on her face nearly broke Beth's heart. 'Really? You mean it? We're going home?'

'Our new home,' Beth said. 'You know we can't go back.'

She watched the hope in Lexi's eyes die and felt the heavy weight of guilt bear down on her shoulders. Had she made the wrong decision coming here?

Trouble in Paradise?

Beth had tried to persuade Lexi to come along on her previous trips, but Lexi was having none of it, hoping, no doubt, that her sister would have a change of heart.

She'd taken loads of photos, but Lexi wouldn't even look at them.

'What's the point?' she'd asked. 'I'm not moving there.'

But here they were.

It had clearly been raining heavily recently because the ditches and dips were full of water, but the road had baked dry in the sun.

They were about to crest the hill and this was the point that Beth imagined Lexi would fall in love just as she had, especially on a day like today with the sky as clear as could be and the sun beating down.

'Get ready, Lexi,' she said. 'Wait till you see this.'

Below them, the little town of Furze Point nestled by the water. Beth glanced at Lexi, but she still looked unimpressed as they began their steady descent towards the town that was to be their new home.

Lexi sat forward and Beth eased off the accelerator, her heart in her mouth. She was banking on this changing Lexi's mind and everything falling perfectly into place.

The first time she saw it, rain had been falling and the sea was invisible in the squall, but still it had felt to Beth as if she was coming home, as if she'd known and loved this place all her life.

The old stone church on the south side of the town was surrounded by a higgledypiggledy array of houses, mainly Georgian but some dating back much further.

Now with it bathed in sunlight and the sea forming a shimmering deep blue backdrop, it looked beautiful.

At the midway point the sails and bunting of the boats in the small marina caught the sun and on the southern edge, the white lighthouse gleamed.

To the east, invisible beyond the trees, was their new home and somewhere buried in there was Scott's Mansion. Beth hadn't seen it, but had been told about it at the second of her interviews.

She waited for Lexi's approval, but nothing was forthcoming. Give her time, she thought. She's eighteen, it's a big change for her on top of so many others. And she is smothered in mud. That's got to feel uncomfortable.

'Could you speed up a bit, please?' Lexi said. 'I want to get out of these clothes.'

'Sorry,' Beth said. 'I was enjoying the view.'

'Unbelievable,' Lexi muttered.

The land narrowed when they reached the bottom of the hill and the single road into town stretched ahead of them.

'Ugh, what's that?'

'Marshes,' Beth said.

'Great. I'm already sick of the mud round here and there's a whole lot more of it.'

Beth ignored that.

'I can't wait to show you around, Lexi. This town has everything. Cliffs, marshes, beaches, shops and a nature reserve to name but a few. If it had a better access road it would be a tourist hotspot.

'There's a lovely lighthouse which has been converted into a café and B and B. I stayed there when I came for my second interview.'

She glanced at Lexi and found her staring at her in disbelief.

'There's an art gallery in town, too,' she added, but it was difficult to inject any enthusiasm into her voice. Lexi seemed determined to hate Furze Point before she'd even seen it and she couldn't have had a worse start.

'I know,' Lexi murmured. 'You told me. Several times.'

The road went in two different directions.

'That's the way into town,' Beth said. 'This way is home.'

'Home,' Lexi snorted. 'This place will never be home. Not for me anyway.'

'We're driving through the nature reserve,' Beth said, still clinging to the hope that Lexi would have a change of heart.

'The wildlife here is amazing — foxes, deer, badgers, squirrels and hedgehogs. I'm told there are seals nearby, too, and porpoises.'

Lexi used to love animals when she was younger, but it seemed even that didn't persuade her.

'Maybe we could get a dog,' Beth said. 'You've always wanted one.'

'For goodness' sake,' Lexi said. 'What's the point? I'll be away at uni most of the time. I probably won't come home in the holidays.

'You get a dog if you want, Beth, but don't pretend you're doing it for me. Don't pretend you're doing any of this for me. It's insulting.'

Beth bit her lip hard to stop herself snapping back. She mustn't cry. It was dangerous to cry when driving, but she felt a whole swell of sorrow building up inside.

The sisters had been so close, but now a huge wedge had been driven between them and the more she tried to get rid of it, the deeper it became embedded, and the worst part was that she'd put it there.

For years Beth had refused to let life beat her down, but she was starting to feel she couldn't fight any more. Her father died when she was twelve and Lexi was two and Beth had to grow up overnight.

Her mum worked all hours and it was up to Beth to keep the home running smoothly, making sure there was food in the fridge and seeing that Lexi got to school on time.

She'd always felt guilty that she'd grown up with a dad and security and Lexi had none of that and she had tried to make it up to her by being the best big sister she could be.

Lexi would never know the fun of riding on Dad's big shoulders or having him run down the road behind her hanging on to her cycle seat.

'I won't let you fall,' he'd yell and he

was right. He never did and when he let go and she was cycling on her own, she'd felt as if she had wings.

Lexi would never know that wonderful, special feeling.

At eighteen Beth left for university and as she hugged Lexi goodbye, she whispered, 'Be a good girl and help Mum, won't you?'

She was only eight, but there were things she could do. Helping out with washing up, making sure her clothes went in the washing tub and just being good. Not that Beth was worried on that score. Lexi was always good.

She was an adorable child, so sweet and loving. It was hard to believe the angry teenager beside her was the same person.

It didn't seem like only ten years ago, but in some ways it felt like a lifetime.

'I don't want you to go, Beth,' Lexi had sobbed as she clung to her. She'd always hated change. Their mum had saved up to take them on holiday to Blackpool once and Lexi had been so homesick, they'd ended up going home after only two days away.

'I'll be back in the holidays,' Lexi promised. 'And I'll e-mail or call you every day.'

'Don't worry about us,' their mother said. 'We're going to be just fine. Mrs Harris will fetch Lexi from school and look after her until I get home from work. She's got my number if she needs to call me.

'That's not to say we won't miss you, darling, but I don't want you worrying about us. You're still young and it's time you had a life of your own.'

Beth had climbed on the coach, her heart heavy yet at the same time she felt as if she was about to embark on the adventure of a lifetime. They blew kisses to each other through the window and it turned out to be the last time Beth ever saw her mum.

She squeezed back tears. Despite the passage of years, sometimes the pain felt so raw.

The student welfare officer had broken

the news. Their neighbour, Mrs Harris, had called the university, not wanting to tell Beth over the phone.

'I'm going to drive you straight home,' the welfare officer said. 'Do you need to get anything?'

'Everything,' Beth had replied woodenly. She knew she wouldn't be coming back. How could she?

Marie Clarke had been late leaving work, in a hurry to get home and pick Lexi up from Mrs Harris. She saw her bus pulling in to the stop on the opposite side of the road and ran for it. That split second that she forgot to check for traffic cost her everything. She'd been killed instantly.

Beth always thought that if she hadn't gone away, her mum wouldn't have been rushing to get home.

Beth had looked after Lexi ever since, getting a job, working all hours just like her mum had and then, just as Lexi was about to go to university, the firm she worked for went bust and Beth found herself without any way of supporting them.

She had precious little in the way of savings and it wasn't long before she was out of money and out of options. Her rent had gone up and she could no longer afford to pay it.

Everyone, it seemed, could only offer part time hours. She took up one post doing six hours a week and when she said she'd have to take on a second job, they told her it was against the terms of her contract. She had to be available to come to work at all times. It seemed so draconian.

'I won't go to uni,' Lexi had said. 'I'll get a job, too. We can manage between us.'

But Beth didn't want Lexi to have to manage. She wanted her to have fun and besides, she was so bright, she'd do well at university.

She'd found information about the job at Furze Point by chance on Facebook and had applied for it on impulse. It was one of those jobs that didn't seem to attract much interest.

They wanted someone to run a shop and café for the people who owned a row of beach houses. During the winter, she'd be responsible for keeping an eye on the houses, doing minor maintenance jobs and getting the places ready for any of the owners that fancied a winter break. And it came with a flat over the shop which was rent free, so even though the job didn't pay much, at least they'd have a roof over their heads and Lexi could afford to stay at university.

All this had happened so quickly. She'd ended up on a shortlist of three and thought she probably had no chance until the call came telling her the job was hers.

The road suddenly curved to the left and the beach was dead ahead. Lexi gasped when she saw it framed by a canopy of trees.

'Pretty good, eh?' Beth said, glancing at her sister. Lexi hadn't been able to hide that she was pleasantly surprised.

'You didn't say we'd be living on the beach,' Lexi said and for a split second, the child she was not so long ago showed through, but then she caught herself. 'How grim,' she added. 'That's going to be fun in winter. Not.'

The road was scattered with sand and it narrowed just as they reached a blue painted wooden building.

'That's it,' Beth said. 'That's home.' It felt like that to her already. She just knew they'd be happy here.

'It looks like a big beach hut.'

'That's why it's called the Beach Hut.' Lexi glared at her.

'I know. I'm not stupid.'

'I know. I'm sorry.'

Further up the road was a small sandy car park. Everything here was sandy.

'I'll move the car up there once we've unloaded it,' Beth said. 'Come on, let's get started.'

The Beach Hut was built on concrete raised several feet above the beach and was bigger than it first appeared.

Beth pushed the back door open and they stepped inside.

'It was unlocked,' Lexi said. 'Is that

safe?'

'Perfectly safe,' a voice said and they turned to see a smart looking man in a navy blazer and pale blue trousers. His hair was white and his face weather-beaten and tanned.

'Welcome, Beth. And you must be Lexi. I've heard all about you.'

He held out his hand and she reluctantly shook it. He pretended not to notice that Lexi was covered in mud and to his credit, he didn't wipe his hand afterwards.

'I'm Tom Bennett. I expect Beth has told you about me. You're off to university, I hear. What are you studying?'

'Art,' Lexi said.

'Wonderful,' he said. 'We have a thriving art community in Furze Point. Every summer we have a week-long festival of art which may interest you.'

'Good for you,' Lexi muttered and Beth clenched her fists at her sides. It was unlike her sister to be so rude, but she didn't want to pick her up on it in case Tom hadn't heard.

'I'm ready to hand the running of this place over to you, Beth. You know where I am if you have any problems. I've told the beach house people not to expect the Beach Hut to be open for a couple of days while you settle in and find your feet as it were.'

'That isn't necessary,' Beth said. She was eager to get started. 'I don't want to inconvenience anyone. I don't see any reason to close at all.'

'Well, it's up to you,' he said. 'Let me just refresh your memory where everything is.'

'That would be great, thank you,' Beth said. 'Lexi, would you like to go upstairs and have a shower? You could take some of your things up to your room.'

'I told you,' Lexi said. 'It's pointless me having a room here since I won't be staying.'

'Well, you'll be staying tonight at least,' Beth said quietly.

'Oh, dear,' Tom said when Lexi had gone. 'Trouble in paradise? I sense your sister isn't happy about moving here. I guess this place takes some getting used to, but I'm sure she'll settle in time. How did she get so muddy?'

'We got stuck in the mud on the way into town,' Beth said. 'A kind stranger towed us out and Beth got sprayed with mud.'

'Wasn't Fergus, was it?' Tom asked. 'Big chap, red hair? He runs the farm shop. He'll do anything for anyone.'

'No, definitely not,' Beth said.

She looked up at the ceiling and sighed.

'I hoped Lexi would fall in love with this place as I did.'

'Don't worry about your sister, Beth,' Tom said. 'She'll settle down and Furze Point has its own magic. It just takes longer to work on some.'

'I'll be glad when she's gone to uni, to be honest,' Beth sighed and felt immediately guilty because she really didn't mean it. In reality, she dreaded Lexi going away.

But in all the years she'd been looking after her sister, she had never been as difficult as she was being now.

'She's bound to be miserable after getting covered in mud,' Tom said. 'We've had a lot of rain and some of these places get very boggy. So who came to your rescue?'

'No idea,' Beth said. 'Tall guy with dark hair and blue eyes. He was driving a newish black 4X4. Aged about thirty.'

She was amazed at just how much she'd noticed. She could even describe what he was wearing, jeans and a plain black T-shirt. Then there was the upward curve of his mouth and the way his eyes twinkled.

Tom looked blank.

'Doesn't ring any bells,' he said. 'Still, it's good he came along when he did, isn't it? I expect you'll see him again, small place like this.'

'I hope so,' she said wistfully, then added quickly, 'I mean I'd like to thank him properly, although I got the impression he was on his way here and changed his mind. He seemed in rather a hurry to get away.'

Tom smiled at her for a moment as if lost in thought, then his eyebrows rose.

'Now,' he said as they went through to the shop and café area, 'if you have time and only if, there's a large cupboard behind the counter.

'I used to clear it out regularly before my back started giving me gyp and Carol has always refused point blank to crawl about in there in case of spiders. I've no idea what's in there, but it would be nice if it were emptied and perhaps put to better use.'

'I'll be glad to do that, Tom,' Beth said.

'If you come across any large sacks of money, they're mine,' Tom said and laughed ruefully.

'If there's anything you can't sell in the shop, you can take it to the monthly car boot sale on the green and donate the proceeds to Tiny Tails. I've already checked with the owners and they approve.'

'Tiny Tails?'

'Our local pet rescue, although why Rachel calls it Tiny Tails I don't know since she rescues anything from monitor lizards to donkeys.'

While he went over everything in the shop with her and answered her questions, she noticed he kept glancing at his watch.

'Why don't you get away now?' she said. 'I'm sure I can manage.'

'Really? Well, Carol is waiting for me, eager to begin our retirement and it starts, apparently, with afternoon tea at the Lighthouse. She booked it weeks ago.'

'Very nice, too,' Beth said.

'You have the number for your contact at the town council, don't you? To be honest, in all the years we've been here, they've never interfered. Always left it to us to run the place. They might come round and do an inspection from time to time, but that's all.'

'Tom,' Beth said, 'don't keep Carol waiting.'

'Oops, no, better not. Toodle-oo, then,' he said and with a cheery wave set off for the car park with a happy bounce in his step.

Beth went to the car and found it empty. Either Lexi had been very busy or they'd been robbed. She decided it had to be the former. Crime was very unusual in Furze Point.

'Lexi! I'm just going to move the car to the car park. I won't be a minute.'

'OK,' Lexi called back. 'Do you want a coffee?'

'Does sand stick to everything?'

Was that a little laugh from Lexi? Oh, Beth hoped so with all her heart. She wanted this to work so much. It had to work. It wasn't ideal and their lives would be very different here, but that could be a good thing.

They were both embarking on new and very different chapters of their lives, but they would always be close, Beth was sure of that. She'd never let anything come between them.

No Time for Regrets

'So this is it then,' Carol said. 'Our retirement officially begins.'

A breeze ruffled her hair and she looked out over the same sea she'd looked out at almost every day of her life. It was never the same from one day to the next though. Today a huge cargo vessel passed by in the distance and closer to shore a yacht sailed leisurely by.

Rosita brought their afternoon tea out on a three-tiered stand with a balloon tied to the top saying: 'Happy Retirement'.

'That looks wonderful!' Carol clapped her hands. 'Thank you, Rosita.'

'I still think you should have had a party,' Rosita said. 'Something special to mark the occasion. We could have held it here or at the sailing club. I bet the beach house owners would hold a barbecue on the beach for you.'

'It's not really us,' Tom said. 'We've never liked big parties or anything like that, have we, Carol?'

'Not really,' Carol said. 'We only had twenty guests at our wedding and that was just the way we liked it.'

She reached out and took Tom's hand, remembering how her dad had wanted to pay for a big wedding. He would have done it somehow and got himself into debt in the process, but they convinced him they just wanted a small celebration.

'Have you got any plans?' Rosita asked. 'A cruise, perhaps? Or a long overdue holiday?'

Carol laughed.

'Every day living here is a holiday,' she said. 'We've no ambition to travel.'

'Well whatever you do I hope you enjoy every well-deserved minute,' Rosita said.

'I'm popping out in a while, but Adriana is here if you want any more of anything and it's all on me. My retirement gift to you.'

'That's so kind, Rosita,' Carol said. 'You already sent us those beautiful flowers.'

'Only because I love you,' Rosita said.

She hugged and kissed them both, then went back inside the Lighthouse.

'Oh, Tom,' Carol said, her voice trembling. 'I'm not sure how much longer I can keep this up. It's getting harder and harder to paste this smile on my face.'

'Don't worry, girl,' Tom said. 'We'll get through it. We always have, haven't we?'

'We should never have bought the bungalow.'

'Don't say that,' Tom said. 'We had to have somewhere to live and as it turned out, it was just as well we bought when we did. We knew if we left it too long we'd never be able to afford a place of our own.'

'We shouldn't have retired.' It had been so hard putting on a brave face for so long, but Carol had grown weary of it. She'd stopped having lunches out with her friends and cancelled her swimming pool membership while Tom had given up golf.

'The beach house people didn't give us a lot of choice, Carol. Neither of us was up to the upkeep side of the job any more, what with my back and your knees. We're a right pair of old crocks, but we'll manage, love.'

Carol was sick of managing, but it looked as if retirement was going to be a bigger struggle than either of them had anticipated.

Buying the bungalow had swallowed up all their savings and their pension pots and they'd still had to take out a mortgage, but they'd expected to be able to carry on working for quite a while longer.

Carol had given up her job as a teaching assistant a few years ago to help Tom out at the Beach Hut and the council had agreed to pay her a small wage, but it wasn't as much as she'd been earning as a TA.

She looked at Tom. He looked so cheerful and full of hope.

He really believed that things would get better for them and Carol didn't want to drag him down today of all days. Besides, he'd always taken care of the financial side of things and he assured her they were fine as long as they were careful.

They'd lived all their married lives at the Beach Hut and had raised their three sons there which hadn't been easy with only two bedrooms and, although there had never been a lot of money to spare, they were happy.

It had been a wonderful place to raise children and they thought they were irreplaceable to the beach house owners, but a retirement they couldn't afford had been forced on them. Carol couldn't help feeling bitter about that.

'These avocado and walnut sandwiches are delicious, Carol,' Tom said, blissfully chewing. 'Try one.'

'You eat them,' Carol said with a smile. 'I'm saving room for those scones and cakes.'

The cargo vessel had passed by and now a huge cruise ship was gliding along the horizon. She had no desire to go on a cruise or fly to more exotic climes, but oh, she wished she could afford to.

They weren't even able to go and stay with their sons any more because of the petrol costs. But there was no point in dwelling on what they couldn't do. They were both in reasonably good health and they still had each other and they had their lovely bungalow which was a dream come true for Carol.

'How did Beth seem?' she asked. 'Keen as ever?'

'Very keen,' Tom said. 'I think the owners will approve of my replacement.'

'Doesn't matter if they don't,' Carol said crisply. 'Not your monkeys, not your circus.'

'What? Monkeys?'

'It's a saying. It means it doesn't have anything to do with you any more. If they don't like it, they can whistle.'

'Carol!'

She couldn't help it. The resentment was bubbling up again. She felt like a saucepan left on too high a heat about to blow its lid. Someone had gone to the council and said that the job was too much for her and Tom.

47

She thought of all they'd done for those people over the years and now they'd been cast aside. She'd even delivered a baby once!

That was a long time ago and the baby was now a teenager, but still, they were always there when needed going above and beyond for the owners of the beach houses.

They'd been cast adrift now they were no longer required. She remembered one of the youngsters telling her about her beloved pony and showing her photos. Oh, how she loved that little horse.

Then the following year she brought photos of a bigger pony and said without so much as a wobble that the smaller one had been sold on.

In the end, that's all she and Tom had meant to the owners. Ponies to be sold on when they outlived their usefulness. Oh, they said they had Carol and Tom's best interests at heart and wanted them to have a wonderful retirement, but they were only looking out for themselves.

Now Beth had arrived to take over,

there was no going back.

'Carol, my love,' Tom said, 'you look as if you've got a mouthful of barnacles.'

'Do I? Sorry. Where were we?' She forced a smile, determined to make herself look on the bright side. And right now they were enjoying an easy afternoon and a delicious tea.

'We were eating this wonderful food,' Tom said. 'Shall I pour you another tea?'

'Go on, then,' she said. She might as well drown her sorrows in tea, but then Rosita appeared with a bottle and two glasses.

'Forget tea,' she said. 'I've got Prosecco.'

'Oh, no,' Tom said. 'No, thank you.'

'Don't be daft,' Rosita said. 'You like it, don't you? It is my gift to you as is this afternoon tea.'

'That's so generous of you, Rosita,' Carol said.

'Bring another glass,' Tom said. 'Come and join us.'

'I think I will,' Rosita said. 'I don't have to leave just yet. Why not?'

★ ★ ★

The flat above the shop had two small bedrooms and an open plan living-room and kitchen. The bedrooms were either side of the living-room and all of the rooms looked out over the sea.

When Beth went upstairs, Lexi was sitting in a chair by the big window. Her hair was still damp from the shower and she looked more relaxed. Two mugs of coffee stood on the table in front of her.

'I need that,' Beth said. 'Thanks, Lexi.'

The flat had the sort of unlived-in but clean smell of a holiday apartment, but Beth could also smell the coffee and the scent of Lexi's shower gel.

Tom and Carol hadn't lived there for some time since buying a bungalow on the other side of town ready for their retirement. Beth wondered fleetingly if she'd still be here when it came time for her to retire.

'What do you think?' she asked. 'I think it's bigger than our old place.'

'It's all right,' Lexi shrugged. 'I'd have

loved it ten years ago, but this place is dead, isn't it? I can't imagine there being any life here. I bet the fair never comes and I don't suppose they have a cinema.'

'Actually, they do. It's an old one that had been derelict for years. The community got together and refurbished it. It might not have the moving seats and three-D effects, but . . .'

Her voice trailed away. Lexi looked less than impressed.

'Do they show talkies yet or is it all silent black and white movies?'

'Don't be facetious, Lexi,' Beth said wearily. 'I'm tired. It was a long difficult drive and we were up early.'

'Don't worry, I'll soon be out of your hair. I heard you telling Tom that you couldn't wait for me to go to uni.'

'That's not what I meant.'

'Why say it, then?'

'Please, Lexi. Don't be like this. Can't we just talk?'

Lexi turned and gazed out at the sea.

Beth sat down and picked up her mug. The view was lovely. You could almost think you were on some tropical beach miles from anywhere. She just wished Furze Point would work the same magic on Lexi as it had on her.

'Why not look on this as a holiday?' Beth said. 'Then you'll be off to university and working hard. At least I hope you'll be working hard.'

'No pressure, then,' Lexi said, but her lips curved into a smile. Beth sat forward and reached for Lexi's hand, reassured that her sister couldn't keep up this angry act for ever.

'We can make this work, Lexi,' she said. 'And wherever you go after university, you'll always know you have this place to come back to.

'Or you could come back and make your life here. Some people live here and work elsewhere. I believe they're talking about getting a ferry service going between here and Stoursley.'

Lexi yawned as if Beth was boring her, but then she had heard it all before. Even Beth was getting fed up repeating herself.

'I might go for a walk. You coming?'

'I'm going to man the shop,' Beth said. 'But you go ahead. If you go that way, you'll see the beach houses. They're all up on stilts.'

'Stilts,' Lexi said scornfully.

Beth stood up at the window and watched Lexi stroll along the beach. She had never felt so far away from her sister.

She missed the closeness they once shared and despite her optimism part of her was afraid they might never get it back.

In some ways it was as if she'd lost Lexi already, unwittingly clearing her out of her life along with all their furniture. As she looked round the flat, she realised there was nothing from their old life here. For the first time, she felt a pang of homesickness.

★ ★ ★

Beth was back downstairs familiarising herself with the stock when she heard footsteps and looked round to see

Rosita from the Lighthouse walking through the open door.

Her dark wavy hair was tied back with a multi-coloured scarf and her brown eyes were dancing as usual. Beth couldn't imagine her ever looking anything but happy.

'Tom said you'd arrived,' she said. 'I thought you might like some food so you don't have to cook this evening after your long journey. It's just frittata and salad with some homemade rolls.'

She put a large plastic container on the counter.

'Welcome,' she said. 'I know you'll be happy here.'

'That's so kind of you, Rosita,' Beth said, brushing away a sudden rush of tears. 'I hadn't even thought about dinner. Now I won't have to.'

'How's your sister?' Rosita asked, looking round. 'Settling in?'

'She's gone for a walk. She's not happy about moving here, I'm afraid.'

'She's young,' Rosita said with a shrug. 'It must seem a very boring place to her, especially coming from a city. It's a lot to get used to.

'Get her to come into town and pop in the Lighthouse and I'll get Adriana to take her under her wing. She can introduce her to some of her friends and perhaps show her this isn't such a dead end place after all.'

'Thank you, Rosita.'

'You come, too. It'll be nice to catch up. I was so pleased when Tom said he'd offered you the job with the blessing of the council and the beach house owners. I thought from the moment I first met you that you'd fit in well here. Ah, this must be Lexi.'

Lexi walked in, her sandals dangling from her fingers, her feet caked in sand and she looked startled to see Rosita.

'Welcome to Furze Point,' Rosita said and hugged Lexi. Beth almost laughed. Lexi looked so surprised, but she instinctively hugged Rosita back.

'It's so lovely to have new faces here. I was just saying to your sister that you should pop into town and visit us at the Lighthouse. My daughter, Adriana can show you round. She's just a year younger than you.'

'That would be nice,' Lexi said politely. 'Thank you. I'm going upstairs now if that's OK. Nice meeting you, Rosita.'

'What a lovely young woman,' Rosita said when Lexi had gone. 'And so beautiful. You're going to miss her when she goes off to uni, aren't you?'

'Very much,' Beth replied. She already missed her and wondered if the real Lexi would ever come back.

★ ★ ★

'What are you doing?' Carol squealed when they got back to the bungalow and Tom suddenly wrapped his arms around her.

'I was going to carry you over the threshold,' he said. 'I know we're not just married, but we're about to embark on an adventure, aren't we?'

'Don't be a fool,' she said trying hard not to laugh. 'Think of your back!'

56

He pulled her into his arms.

'Carol, I don't want you to worry about money, OK? Haven't I always looked after you? We've always got through things together.'

He was right. There had been tough times. When their middle son, Simon, was ill as a child and had been rushed to hospital by ambulance with suspected meningitis, the people from the beach houses had rallied round.

Carol had gone in the ambulance with Simon, and Tom turned up at the hospital soon after in a sports car driven by a top cardiac surgeon who owned one of the beach houses.

'Don't you worry about a thing,' William had said. 'We'll take care of your boys and the Beach Hut and one of us will pick the three of you up when Simon is better and ready to come home.'

And he'd spoken to people at the hospital on their behalf, asking all the right questions and getting the answers Carol and Tom so desperately needed.

Oh, gosh, thinking about that washed

a lot of the bitterness away. It was so easy to forget the good things that happened.

And really, no-one had told them to go out and buy a pretty detached bungalow.

They could have easily found something smaller and cheaper, but they'd fallen in love with this one with its view of the sea and beautiful garden.

Taking out a mortgage had been their biggest mistake. Their sons had all advised against it, but Carol and Tom had been caught up in the excitement of it all and hadn't heeded their advice.

At the time, although they'd known retirement was on the horizon, they thought they had a few working years left. Property prices were constantly rising, so they had thought it best to buy when they did.

If things were looking bleak now it wasn't because of the beach house owners or sudden retirement, but because they had been foolish to assume anything, Carol thought. They were just going to have to tighten their belts. Carol had every intention of seeing if she could go back to work as a teaching assistant.

They had too much to be happy about to let a stupid thing like lack of money spoil things for them. She was going to take a leaf out of her husband's book and view everything with a positive eye.

New Beginnings

The following day, Lexi came downstairs in white shorts and a yellow T-shirt and said she was going to walk into town.

'I can give you a lift,' Beth offered.

'It's all right. I'm going to make a day of it. I might pop in the Lighthouse. I just follow the footpath along the coast, right?'

'That's right, love,' Beth said. 'It's quite a long walk. If you get tired, give me a call and I'll pick you up. Be sure to check out the art gallery, too.'

Beth was kept busy making packed lunches for people going out on their boats and others who just popped in for a coffee. She suspected they'd come in to have a look at the new manager of the Beach Hut and see if they approved of Tom's choice.

'Well, you're a lot prettier than old Tom,' one man said and his wife glared at him.

'That's so sexist,' she said. 'I do apologise, Beth.'

'I took it as a compliment,' Beth said, laughing. She couldn't remember the last time anyone had said she was pretty.

Lexi was the pretty one with her big grey eyes and straight silky fair hair while Beth's eyes were mossy green and her hair never seemed to look tidy no matter how much time she spent on it.

'One I'm sure you get all the time,' the lady said. 'And Ed's right, you are definitely prettier than old Tom.'

Every time someone came in, Beth's heart gave an odd little leap followed by a shred of disappointment when it turned out not to be her rescuer. Although what he'd be doing coming here she didn't know.

Lexi didn't get home until the evening.

'Did you have a good day?' Beth asked. 'Where did you go?'

'Everywhere,' Lexi said. 'I met loads of people. Don't get your hopes up though, Beth. I can't see me ever settling here.'

'So you keep telling me,' Beth said, but she was quietly hopeful.

Rosita's daughter Adriana was a lovely

girl, like a younger version of her mother. It wouldn't take long for Lexi to warm to the town once she let her guard down and stopped feeling so sorry for herself.

* * *

Three weeks later, Beth was loading up the car again, this time to take Lexi to university.

Since they'd arrived, Lexi had spent a lot of time out and about. When Beth finally had the time to visit Rosita at the Lighthouse, she thanked her for suggesting that Lexi should meet Adriana, but Rosita just shook her head.

'She's never been here,' she said. 'I don't know who she's meeting, but it isn't Adriana.'

Lexi was disappointed, but also pleased that Lexi was making friends on her own.

She asked about them, but Lexi wasn't forthcoming on that front. She'd helped in the shop, too, when they were busy, but things weren't the same between them and Beth felt as if she was for ever treading on eggshells.

Every day Lexi remarked on something she missed from their old home, from the saggy old sofa to the ancient clock on the hall wall which was always several minutes out one way or the other.

The owners of the beach houses seemed friendly and welcoming. One couple had phoned asking her to get their house ready for their arrival and they'd tipped her handsomely for the good job she'd done cleaning the place up and stocking up their fridge and cupboards.

The beach houses themselves were really something else. Beth had never seen anything like them before. They were all on stilts with decking areas big enough to seat several people round a table and they were spacious inside and rather luxurious.

The backs of the houses were built into the hill so the owners just had to step out of their back doors into small gardens which led on to the road.

'By the way,' Lexi said, breaking into Beth's thoughts, 'I found that mansion you told me about.'

'Did you?'

'It's at the far end of the beach, way past the beach houses just before you come to a deep creek. You follow a steep path up the hill and it takes you right into the grounds.'

'That's amazing,' Beth said. 'The road to it seems impassable.'

'Yes, it is. I tried going that way but there are some trees down. Must have been there for years. Can you imagine leaving a house to go to ruin like that?'

'Is it ruined?'

'It's a wreck. Some of the windows are broken. It'd be lovely to live there though. It's huge.'

'Might be better to keep away from it,' Beth said. 'It might be unsafe.'

'It has stables out the back and massive overgrown gardens,' Lexi went on. 'It must have been really grand once. I was just saying because I don't think you should go up there. It's a shame it's been left to ruin, though, when people are homeless.'

'Yes, it doesn't seem right, but things are different here. You never see people living on the streets like we did at home.'

'Didn't you know there was a homeless man in Furze Point?'

'No,' Beth said. 'I didn't.'

'Well, there is. He sleeps in the nature reserve in a tent. It's not right, is it?'

'No,' Beth agreed.

'So this place isn't quite the utopia you think it is,' Lexi added. 'The people aren't all perfect. They're flawed just the same as the people anywhere else and you should be careful. I think you're trusting strangers far too readily.'

'I'll be careful,' Beth said, frowning. What on earth was Lexi talking about?

'Whatever Tom says about it being safe here, you should keep the doors locked.'

'I will. I do.' Beth was touched that her sister was worried about her, but wishing she wasn't.

'That's the lot,' Lexi said as she slung her backpack into the boot. 'I'm ready to go. So you'll lock up at night and you'll keep away from that old house? I know you're going to end up with time on your hands over the winter. You might be tempted.'

'I won't be. I'm going to miss you, Lexi,' Beth said.

'Yeah, right.'

'I love you. You know that.'

She went to hug her, but Lexi ducked out of the way and slipped into the front seat of the car.

'Let's go,' she said. 'The sooner we're away from this dump the better.'

Beth felt stung. This dump, as she called it, was their new home and the people, flawed or not, had taken them to their hearts.

* * *

Tom and Carol were going to man the Beach Hut until Beth got back and Tom was serving a customer while Carol came out to see them off.

Carol often popped in to see how they

were doing and occasionally she'd lend a hand in the shop as if she couldn't keep away from the place.

'Give her time,' she whispered as she hugged Beth. 'She'll come round. I had similar problems with one of my boys. The others went through teenage rebellion much younger, but Simon waited until he was eighteen, then he was a nightmare, but it didn't last long. You just have to wait for it to pass and be there when they come out the other side.'

She bobbed down and waved at Lexi.

'Have a wonderful time, sweetheart,' she said. 'Don't do anything I wouldn't do.'

Lexi smiled and waved back and a few minutes later they were off, heading along the winding road which would take them inland and back to the hustle and bustle of everyday life.

Beth pulled carefully into a passing space to let a petrol tanker and a delivery lorry come through and Lexi's breath hissed through her teeth as she gripped her seat.

'I thought they were going to hit us. You seem to be not going far enough into the sides now.'

'Not even close,' Beth said. 'It looks worse from the passenger side.'

The conversation between them boiled down to small talk. It was as if they were strangers. Beth didn't want to say goodbye to her sister on that note, but couldn't think of any way to bridge the gap between them.

* * *

The halls were busy with several people arriving and others saying goodbye. Lexi was the last to arrive in the flat she was sharing with three other girls and two boys.

The others introduced themselves and a small, dark-haired girl called Anja asked Beth for her contact details.

'We're going to look out for each other,' she said.

'Spy on each other you mean?' Lexi said, bristling.

'No, of course not. But if something happens and we need to contact your sister, we'll have her number.'

'I think it's a wonderful idea,' Beth said. 'You're going to be like a family, all living together, helping each other out and I feel better knowing what a friendly lot you are. When I . . . ' She stopped herself.

Now wasn't the time to remember how kind everyone had been when her mum died. Her flatmates had rallied round, helping her pack, giving her hugs, promising their support. But she'd lost touch with them all. They'd assumed she was coming back, but of course she couldn't.

She'd never forgotten the friendships she'd forged so quickly and how much they'd meant to her even for so short a time.

Hopefully the same thing would happen for Lexi without her time being cut short.

'I'll give you my number, too,' Anja said. 'So if you have any concerns, you can call me.'

'For goodness' sake, why would my sister have any concerns? I don't need a minder,' Lexi said. 'In case you hadn't noticed, we're all adults here.' She turned and stomped off to her room and Beth almost laughed because she wasn't acting much like an adult right now.

'She's tired,' Beth said apologetically. 'And she's been through some upheaval lately. I'll give you my number anyway, Anja. I think it's a good idea and I'm sure Lexi will, too, when she's had time to think about it.'

Lexi was sitting on her bed in her room when Beth joined her.

'I hope you're not going to give that girl your number. Who does she think she is, anyway?'

'I think she's just trying to be friendly, Lexi,' Beth said. 'You've got to give people a chance. You'll make lots of new friends if you're open with people.'

'I don't need friends. I've got friends.'

Sometimes Beth thought Lexi was more mature when she was twelve than she was now. It was as if she'd regressed.

When it was time to leave, Lexi came down to see Beth off. She still seemed quiet and moody, but Beth hoped the others would bring her out of her shell and find the real Lexi hiding beneath.

'Well, this is it then,' Beth said. 'Call me if you need me, any time, day or night. I can be here in a few hours.'

'Unless you get stuck behind a tractor or down in a ditch on that awful road,' Lexi said with a ghost of a smile that reminded Beth that her sister was still in there somewhere.

'I'll try not to.' She laughed. 'Seriously, though, if you need me, I'll drive right over the top of any tractors that get in my way.'

'Don't say that,' Lexi said, the smile fading as quickly as it had come. 'Please drive carefully. I can't lose you, too, Beth.'

'Oh, love, you're not going to lose me, I promise,' Beth said, wrapping her arms round her little sister.

Lexi hesitated before hugging her back and tears sprang to Beth's eyes. She hadn't had a hug and barely any smiles since she'd told Lexi about the job and the move.

She had spent the past few weeks torn between thinking she was making an awful mistake and that this could quite possibly turn out to be the best thing she'd ever done. All she was waiting for was Lexi's stamp of approval.

'Make sure you eat properly,' Beth said, holding Lexi at arm's length. 'Drink plenty of water so you don't get head-aches and try to eat fruit every day.'

'OK,' Lexi said.

'Don't let anyone persuade you to do anything you're uncomfortable with, don't ever leave your drinks unattended and do keep in touch.'

Beth tried to remember all the things she'd wanted to talk to Lexi about, but her mind had gone blank.

'I'll be fine,' Lexi said. 'Call me when you get home or send a text or some-thing.'

'I will and you promise to call me every day or e-mail, even if it's just an emoji so

I know you're OK.'

They hugged again and heart full, Beth got in her car and drove off, watching Lexi grow smaller and smaller in her rear view mirror until she turned the corner, pulled in and sobbed her heart out at the side of the road.

She was crying because Lexi cared that she got home OK and wanted her to drive carefully. Recently she'd felt as if Lexi didn't like her at all and now she knew that wasn't true.

She grabbed a handful of tissues, mopped her eyes and blew her nose. This was going to turn out fine, she just knew it.

Back at the Beach House, Tom was busy counting the day's takings while Carol tidied up.

'I've enjoyed myself today, Tom,' Carol said. 'But it's reminded me how tiring this job was. I'm certainly glad we won't be here for another winter, checking on the beach houses and battening down the hatches when the storms come.'

'Definitely,' Tom said. 'I just hope

Beth is up to all that.'

'Ooh, Tom, you're treading dangerous ground there. Just because she's a woman doesn't make her incapable and you said yourself she seemed very competent. That's why you chose her.

'Remember that winter you had pneumonia? Who kept everything going? I even managed to fix the Stephenson's temperamental old generator.'

'Yes, but we always had each other, Carol. Beth's on her own. Ideally I'd have taken on a married couple, but Beth was the best person for the job.'

'Well, we'll be here if she needs us,' Carol said. 'And perhaps Lexi will help out in the holidays.'

'You think?' Tom looked doubtful. 'She seems to have well and truly taken against Furze Point.'

'It's not for everyone,' Carol said. 'None of our boys settled here.'

'No, but we did.' Tom grinned. 'And I haven't regretted it for a moment. All we can do with Lexi is make her welcome.'

'I've tried. She seems like a sweet girl

74

underneath that prickly façade. It must be a worry for Beth, though.'

'Shall we lock up and go home?' Tom asked.

'I'd rather wait for Beth to get back, if you don't mind. See that she's home safe.'

'I thought you'd say that,' Tom said. 'It's fine with me. You're fond of her already, aren't you?'

'Well, aren't you?'

'I am. She's perfect for this place as were we.'

'Tom, there's something I have to tell you.'

'Oh, sounds serious.'

'Not really. I've got a job, starting next week.'

'A job? But we've retired.' He looked dismayed.

'I'm going to be helping Rosita at the Lighthouse,' she said. 'She wants Adriana to concentrate more on her studies and she'll be off to university next year.'

'No,' Tom said.

'No?' Carol laughed incredulously.

'I'm not having you working there, going up and down those stairs and running in and out with sandwiches and tea. It's not on, Carol.'

Carol hugged him, glad that he still loved her enough to care.

'I won't be doing any of those things. I'll be working behind the scenes, making sandwiches, making the tea and loading the dishwasher. It's all stuff I can do standing on my head and Rosita is going to pay me more than minimum wage. It'll help, won't it, Tom?'

His jaw set rigidly and he stared out of the window at the sea, a muscle twitching in his cheek. If she could see his male pride, she was sure it would have a huge dent in it, but dents could always be coaxed out.

'Tom,' she said. 'It'll be an income and just means we can get straight quicker.'

'I've always looked after us, Carol,' he said at last. 'What will people think? What sort of husband am I?'

'I don't care what people think,' Carol said. 'But if anyone asks, I shall say I'm doing it because I'm bored and I miss the Beach Hut.

'And you're a wonderful husband. Come on.' She nudged him cheerfully. 'Get a couple of chairs out and I'll make us a drink. We can sit out the front there and pretend we're waiting for the boys to come home from school.'

'Well, I suppose if you're working, we might be able to afford some luxuries,' Tom said, clearly warming to the idea. Carol smiled sadly. They were quite a long way from being able to afford luxuries.

Sitting out on the beach, Carol tried to pretend they didn't have money worries. It would be worse in the middle of the night when she woke up in a cold sweat, worried out of her mind.

Things always seemed worse in the small hours, but even telling herself that didn't help her get back to sleep. Hopefully after their busy day, she would sleep through.

It was dark before they heard a car driving up the road behind the Beach

Hut heading for the car park.

'That will be Beth,' Carol said, sounding relieved and Tom chuckled. 'What's so funny, Tom?'

'Just thinking of all the times we sat out here in the dark watching the moon shimmer on the sea waiting to hear one or other of the boys coming home. Remember when Andrew got the motorcycle?'

'Don't remind me,' Carol said. 'That's when my hair started turning white. I'll never forget the night he came off it. It's a miracle he wasn't killed.'

'He almost was,' Tom said, deadpan. 'Once you saw he was still in one piece, I thought you were going to kill him!'

Beth appeared, a bemused smile on her face.

'What are you two still doing here?' she said. 'I thought you'd have gone home ages ago. It's getting late.'

'Oh, just chewing the fat,' Carol said. 'Remembering times past. How was Lexi?'

'Fine,' Beth said. 'She has a lovely room and her flatmates seem really nice.'

'That's good. And the drive was OK?'

'Not too bad. I was stuck in a queue for an hour coming back because they closed two lanes on the motorway, but apart from that it was all good. I didn't have time to stop to eat though. Have you two had anything?'

'No,' Tom said, looking surprised. 'We haven't.'

'We forgot all about eating,' Carol said. 'How silly.'

'Come upstairs,' Beth said. 'I'll cook a bit extra and we can eat together. Please say yes. You'd be doing me a favour. I'm feeling a bit lost at the moment.'

'In that case, we'd love to,' Carol said and while Tom put the chairs away, Carol followed Beth up to the flat that had been her home for so many years.

A Problem Shared

'That's good. And the drive was OK? for an hour coming back because they

The days grew shorter and the nights longer and soon the beach house people were winding up for the season, packing up and going home. Some sailed straight from the marina in their boats, others left in their cars. Only a few stragglers remained, reluctant, it seemed, to let go of the summer, especially as it had given them one last blast of heat just when they thought it was all over.

There was a definite chill of autumn in the air and yet out of the wind, the sun still brushed your skin with warmth. The owners came by the Beach Hut before leaving, handing keys to Beth and giving her lists of things they wanted doing over the winter, anything from a bit of painting to letting workmen in and supervising as they installed new bathrooms or fitted wardrobes. Some of the houses needed specialist repair work and Beth would arrange that, too.

A few people planned to spend Christmas here and wanted her to stock the cupboards and fridges for the holidays when the time came.

She was looking forward to Christmas. Lexi would be home and Beth planned to make it a Christmas to remember, their first in their new home.

She leaned on the counter and rested her chin on her hands. The sea was bluer than ever now it was turning colder, and the gulls seemed louder than they had a few weeks before.

She still hoped the guy they'd met on the road coming here would walk through that door one day and she laughed at herself for entertaining such wistful thoughts.

Lexi didn't contact Beth every day as she'd promised, but Beth learned to live with that. She was bound to be busy with studying and hopefully with her new friends, although she didn't say much about them.

She didn't say much about anything if they spoke on the phone and they were back to making small talk.

The doors to the shop were propped open and she saw a couple of youths walking along the sand. Every so often they'd stop and skim stones across the water. She straightened up and watched them walk past, the skin at the back of her neck prickling.

'How ridiculous,' she told herself. It was just that they looked wrong and out of place, as if they were lurking rather than out for a walk. They didn't even have a dog as far as Beth could see.

She remembered what Tom had said about there being very little crime in the town and decided she was being paranoid.

She also remembered what he'd said about the beach houses containing a lot of valuable stuff and now she was responsible for their security. Then there was Lexi telling her to make sure the door was locked.

Stepping outside, she watched them stop further along where the beach houses began. They looked up at the houses, then turned back. Had they been sizing them up?

'Hi,' she said as they walked past, wanting to let them know they'd been noticed. 'Making the most of the good weather?'

'Yeah,' one of them grunted as he pulled his hood further up. They were probably about Lexi's age, but could have been a lot younger. It was hard to tell. Once they were past, they laughed. Watching them slouch away back towards town, Beth pondered on her own lost youth.

She'd had boyfriends, but never anything serious. How could she? There had been one, once, that she'd really liked, but when he found out she was looking after a younger sister, he scarpered. Besides that, she just didn't have time in her life for romance and now look at her, pushing thirty and still single with very little chance of that changing and she was very unlikely to meet anyone here.

The owners of the beach houses were either much older than her or already married with kids. If she let herself think about it, she would have liked to have had a family, but some things just weren't meant to be.

Maybe that was what Lexi was afraid of, ending up like Beth.

★　★　★

By the end of the week everyone had gone and Beth hadn't heard from Lexi for days. She'd been busy with people leaving and once it was quiet, she was left with her thoughts and they weren't happy ones.

Lexi wasn't answering her phone and was ignoring her texts. Beth had no choice but to call Anja.

'Actually, I've been hoping you'd ring,' Anja said. 'I've been debating whether to call you. The others said not to interfere, but I'm worried about Lexi.'

'Is she all right?' Beth's stomach clenched.

'I was hoping you'd tell me. She hasn't been turning up for lectures,' Anja said. 'Then this guy turned up. She said he was her boyfriend. He hung around here for a while and our flatmates didn't like it. He took some of our food. We spoke to Lexi about it and she went home in a huff. We really didn't mean to upset her.'

'Lexi doesn't have a boyfriend,' Beth said. 'And she's not home.'

She'd never shown much interest in boys. At school she'd been so buried in work and driven by her determination to do well that she eschewed the party scene. She didn't even go clothes shopping, for heaven's sake. Beth had worried that Lexi was missing out on fun and now she'd gone completely the other way, living a life Beth knew nothing about.

'She's not?' Anja said. 'But I'm sure that's where she said she was heading. She's been gone over a week.'

Beth was shaking when she ended the call. Where on earth could Lexi be? She didn't think of this as home anyway and it was probably the last place she'd come.

Home was where they used to live.

She sent Lexi a text.

'I know you're not at university. I'm

worried. Please let me know you're OK. I love you.'

An hour later her phone beeped and she snatched it up, relieved when she saw she had a text from Lexi.

'I'm fine. Don't worry. I'll go back when I'm ready. Maybe.'

'Has something happened?' Beth texted back. 'Please answer your phone so we can talk, Lexi. Are you in trouble?'

'Not in trouble. Having fun. Signal bad. No point phoning.'

'What was Mum's first name?'

'What? Marie, of course. Why?'

'Just checking.'

Beth hoped if Lexi was in real trouble, she would have replied with the wrong name. It always worked in the movies anyway.

'Where are you? Anja said you'd gone home.'

'I don't have a home any more,' Lexi replied which left Beth in no doubt that she was talking to her sister.

'Keep in touch,' she answered. 'I love you, Lexi.'

She didn't get a reply and tossed the phone aside not knowing what was worse, the hurt or the anger. At Lexi's age, she had already taken responsibility for her little sister, yet Lexi was acting like a rebellious teenager or worse, a spoilt child.

All because she didn't want to move.

She paced up and down, wringing her hands together. She'd never felt so helpless in her life. If only she knew where Lexi was so she could at least talk to her face to face.

She desperately needed to keep busy and remembered that Tom had asked her to clear out the cupboard behind the main counter when things got quieter. It was about three feet high and went back a long way under another counter with shelving over the top.

Now was as good a time to start as any. She pulled open the two doors and gasped. The cupboard was packed with stuff. The first thing she pulled out was a pair of roller boots. She laughed. Tom said they tried to sell everything in the little shop. He wasn't kidding.

There was a box of bathing hats, half a dozen snorkels and a packet of old-fashioned wooden clothes pegs. It was like a treasure trove, but the cupboard could be put to better use and perhaps some of this stuff would sell at a boot sale if not in the shop.

After a while there was enough space made for her to crawl inside. She could see why Tom and Carol didn't want to do it. She shone her torch around, terrified a spider would be startled by the light and drop on her head.

She found umbrellas, a wind break and several pairs of plastic sandals, a box of nails, a set of saucepans and a folding chair. There were greetings cards, rubber gloves and a socket set.

She was buried deep in the cupboard when she heard the bell above the door jangle. She'd forgotten to lock it!

'Lexi!' she said and began to reverse at speed, terrified her sister would walk in and walk straight out again.

'Sorry,' a male voice said. 'Don't rush,

you might . . .'

She tried to straighten up too soon and hit her head on the top of the cupboard. For a moment pain seemed to melt over her scalp, crawling down her face and making her eyes sting and water.

'. . . bang your head,' the voice said as the fog cleared.

She heard the counter flap open then a hand rested on her back.

'Are you OK? Back up slowly. Easy now. It's OK, you're clear.'

She felt such an idiot as she crawled backwards and into the light, but there was something familiar and comforting about the voice.

'I'm sorry,' she said rocking back on to her heels. 'I was just sorting out the cupboard. I wasn't expecting anyone in this late and I thought you were . . . never mind. How can I help you?'

'I think you're the one that needs help at the moment,' he said, gently pulling her to her feet. 'Can you walk? Come and sit down. I'll get some ice for your head. Hold on, it's you, isn't it?'

She blinked up at him. Those blue eyes!

'You've come to my rescue again,' she said, smiling. 'Are you real?'

'I don't know about rescuing you,' he said. 'Since it's my fault you banged your head, but yes, I am real.'

He led her to the small café area and she sank on to a chair. It was dark outside and the moon was shining on the sea. She hadn't realised how much time had elapsed since she started clearing out the cupboard.

He checked the freezer and found some ice which he wrapped in a clean tea towel.

Gently parting her hair, he looked at her head, running his fingers over her tender scalp.

'No dents,' he said. 'That's good.'

'Is it?'

'You've grazed your back of your head a little. Hold the ice on. It'll help. Can I get you a drink?'

'Water, please,' she said. She watched him go over to the fridge, amazed and

90

rather pleased to see him again. But what was he doing here? She wondered if she'd knocked herself out and was dreaming, but there was nothing dreamlike about her sore head.

'Sorry, I should have said, I'm Noah Walsh.'

'Pleased to meet you, Noah Walsh,' Beth said. 'I'm Beth Clarke, the manager here. Were you looking for anything in particular?'

He grinned.

'Pleased to meet you too, Beth Clarke,' he said. 'I was just heading back to town. I'm staying at the Lighthouse for the time being, but I'll need a torch, candles and matches to start with and as I recall, this shop sold just about everything from emergency ice-lollies to thermal socks.' He sat down and looked round the shop. 'You do sleeping bags! I'll probably need one of those too.'

'Emergency ice-lollies?' she repeated, laughing.

'When you're nine and hot and sticky, getting an ice-lolly is an emergency,' he said and she laughed.

She'd certainly come to understand why the Beach Hut was a public amenity. It wasn't just there for the beach house people.

'You came back after all,' she said. 'Last time I saw you, you said you hadn't got any further than Bluebell Farm before getting cold feet. I guess this is one of those places that draws you back. Are you from one of the beach houses? Is there a problem with your generator? How long have you been at Furze Point?'

'Whoa, so many questions.' He laughed. 'No, I'm not from one of the beach houses, don't worry,' he said. 'I was walking along the beach and I saw the lights on and thought I'd pop in.

'I haven't been here since I was a kid, but it doesn't seem to have changed.' He looked round the shop. 'It's like stepping back in time. I take it Tom and Carol have retired by now?'

'Just this year,' Beth said. 'Did you have one of the beach houses years ago?'

'No. My gran lived here and I used

to come for the holidays. The last time I must have been about nine or ten. Then my parents moved to Cape Town and we just didn't come back.

'I think there had been a falling out to be honest because when I was about eighteen and planning to come back, they told me Gran had died.'

A shadow crossed his face as he remembered something that obviously still hurt him.

'But you don't want to hear about all that,' he said. 'How's your head?'

'Sore,' she said. 'I'm sorry about your gran. You must have been very close.'

'We were. Her letters stopped when I was about fourteen and I guess that's when she died. My parents let me think she'd lost interest in me. I should have known that wasn't true. It seemed pointless to come back when I found out she wasn't here.

'This year is the first time I've been in the UK since we left when I was a kid. To be honest, this feels more like home than any of the other places I've lived. We were in Cape Town for three years, then Dad's work took him to Hong Kong.

'We never settled anywhere more than a few years and now my parents have retired and are living in India although I wouldn't put it past them to get itchy feet again.' He laughed softly. 'How about you, Beth Clarke? What's your story?'

'I'm more interested in yours,' she said. 'Where have you been since that day you pulled us out of the ditch?'

'Staying in London with friends,' he said. 'Then I thought I should man up and just come here and face the demons I didn't even know I had. How's your sister? Still angry at the world?'

Beth found herself telling him. It seemed only fair since he'd confided in her. She sensed another lonely soul and thought it was awful that his parents had let their argument come between Noah and his grandmother.

'You must be so worried. But you had to cope on your own when she was growing up?' he said when she'd finished. 'No grandparents or aunts and uncles to help?'

'My parents grew up and met in foster care, so no, no family that I know of. You were lucky to have your wonderful grandmother even if it was for a short time. How about you, is there any other family?'

'I don't have any siblings,' he said. 'I sometimes think life would have been better if I had and I've always said if I had kids, I'd never have just one.'

'I've never really thought about it,' Beth said wistfully. 'I mean I've thought it would be nice to have a family one day, but I certainly hadn't got round to thinking of numbers.'

It was amazing how easy it was to talk to Noah and in some ways Beth felt as if she'd known him for ages, but that might be because she'd thought about him so much over the past few weeks. But he was probably just passing through, staying for a while to remember his gran before moving on again.

'How's the head now? No double vision or feeling sick or anything?'

'Just feels bruised and I feel silly.'

'Don't feel silly. I made you jump. It was entirely my fault. I'm going to get back to town now before Rosita thinks I've got lost and sends out a search party. I might have to buy a torch, though, as I'll be walking along the coastal path. And I'll give you my number. If you start to feel dizzy or ill at all, call me.'

'I can give you a lift back to town,' Beth offered.

'I don't think you should be driving. Just give me a call in the morning, let me know you're OK. I'll be coming in for supplies anyway later in the day.' He stood to leave. 'Sure you're OK?'

She smiled. His concern was genuine and it felt rather nice to have someone care.

'Absolutely,' she said.

When he'd gone, she locked the shop and headed up to the flat. She could finish clearing out the cupboard in the morning.

As she entered the small hallway at the top of the stairs, she caught sight of herself in the mirror. The first thing that struck her was that she was smiling, the second thing was her curls all dusty and full of cobwebs and her face smeared with dirt. She groaned. Wasn't that typical?

Plans Afoot

Carol reversed through the front door of the bungalow and shook her umbrella to get rid of the worst of the rain.

'Tom!' she shouted. 'Tom! Are you here?'

'Of course I'm here,' he said, emerging from the kitchen with his sleeves rolled up and flour up to his elbows. 'What are you doing home? I thought you were doing the beds up at the Lighthouse and staying there for the lunchtime shift.'

She stopped in her tracks, dripping all over the floor.

'What are you doing, Tom?'

'I'm making a crumble.'

'Why?' She shook her head. What a silly question. It didn't matter why Tom had taken it into his head to make a crumble. 'Never mind. Tom, there's a guest staying at the Lighthouse. I saw him having his breakfast.'

'A guest, eh?' Tom crossed his arms. 'Well, yes, that's because it's a B and B, love, you know that.'

'Yes, yes, I know all that.'

'It'd be a funny old do if they didn't have any guests.'

'Stop teasing, Tom! It's who the guest is. I mean it could be a coincidence, but I don't think it is. I'm sure it isn't. I just can't believe he's back.

'I asked Rosita what his name is and she told me without turning a hair, but she only moved here a few years ago so she wouldn't know.'

'Wouldn't know what? You're not making any sense. Look, come on through, I want to get my crumble in the oven.'

'Why are you making a crumble, Tom?'

'I popped in the Bluebell Farm shop and Fergus had these lovely big fat cooking apples and I thought how much I fancied an apple crumble and I was going to ask you to make one, but then I thought it's not fair when you're working.

'Anyway, I thought I could cook dinner and we could have apple crumble for dessert.'

'You're cooking dinner? And you're planning it now? At this time of the morning?'

'It was supposed to be a surprise,' Tom said. 'But that ship sailed the minute you came in the door. I was planning a nice afternoon out after you finished work. Cinema if it was raining or a stroll along the prom if the sun came out, then home here for dinner cooked by me.'

'Oh, Tom.' Carol's lip wobbled.

He'd always been a bit of a disaster in the kitchen and after the time he boiled her best saucepan dry and incinerated the fish fingers and very nearly the Beach Hut as well, he'd vowed to stay out of the kitchen.

He was fine making sandwiches or anything like that, but he tended to keep away from the oven. She was so touched that she almost forgot why she'd come rushing home.

'It looks lovely, Tom,' she said as he grabbed the oven gloves and popped the crumble in the oven and she subtly checked the oven temperature — which was fine. 'Just a minute . . . Are you buttering me up for something?'

His cheeks were pink from the blast of heat from the oven, but they turned fiery red.

'What are you up to, Tom? You'd better tell me right now.'

'I'm not up to anything,' he said, his voice going up a notch, a sure sign that he was hiding something.

'And what's this about the cinema? We can't afford fripperies like that.'

'It's seniors' day and we're seniors. It's really only a couple of quid each.'

'Couple of quid?'

'Well, six, but it's not bad, is it?'

She pulled out a chair and sat down.

'Well I'm not going back to the Lighthouse until you tell me what you're up to and if I'm not back in time for lunch Rosita might give me the sack and then where will we be?'

'Rosita won't . . . ' he began, but then he sighed and slumped down in the chair opposite. 'It was supposed to be a surprise.'

'You're not talking about dinner, are you? Oh, Tom, what have you done?'

'Nothing drastic,' he said, lifting his hands up. 'Something we've talked about for years, but for some reason never got round to doing.

'It's not set in stone or anything and we can change our minds if you really don't want to do it.'

Carol groaned. Tom was a rare one for skirting all round the point without actually getting there.

'Tom, what have you done?' Carol demanded.

'Let me make you a coffee,' he said.

'Tom!'

'I was driving home the other day and I went past Tiny Tails and I thought a dog would be nice. It would get us — me — out of the house and so I popped in and spoke to Rachel.'

'A dog! Tom, are you serious? How can we afford a dog? We can barely afford to feed ourselves and then you've got vet bills and insurance as well as the food and all the other bits and pieces we'd need. I'm sorry, Tom, but no. It's not happening.'

She was so cross, she could hardly bring herself to look at him. What on earth had happened to her husband lately? He used to be so careful and it seemed he couldn't spend their money fast enough.

'Don't be mad, Carol,' he said.

'Mad? You don't know the half of it. I'm going back to work.'

She stood up and had to bite back tears as the sight of Tom's stricken face. He looked so disappointed and upset.

'I thought you'd like a dog,' he said.

'I would. I'd love one, but how many times do I have to say it? We can't afford it.'

'Maybe we can,' he said. 'You're not the only one with a job. I've got a little earner myself.'

'Doing what?'

'I'm going to walk dogs for people and also when they go away on holiday, I'm going to pop in and feed their cats and any other small pets. It pays really well

103

and I'll enjoy it.

'I've got myself a Facebook page all set up and I've had several enquiries. I thought it was something we could do together and if it takes off, you might be able to give up working at the Lighthouse. What do you think?'

'I think . . . well, I don't know what to think, Tom. On the face of it, it sounds like a wonderful idea for a business. As for a dog for us, Rachel surely wasn't going to just hand over one without speaking to both of us first.'

'Of course not. She's going to nip round to speak to us about it and make sure we're both committed to the idea. I was going to tell you tonight over dinner.

'It was when I was talking to her that I had the idea of becoming a dog walker. She said so many people have to surrender their pets because their circumstances change and they have to go out to work or work away or simply aren't well. It must be heartbreaking to have to do that.'

'It really must,' Carol murmured.

'Look at the time. I must get back. I promise I'll think it over, Tom.'

She headed for the door. The crumble was already starting to smell nice as it cooked.

'Hold on,' Tom called out. 'You came home to tell me something.'

'Oh, yes,' she said. 'I completely forgot.'

'So who is Rosita's mystery guest?'

'It's Noah,' she said. 'Noah Walsh.'

'Noah? After all this time?' Tom's eyes hardened and his voice was brittle. 'What does he want?'

'I have no idea, but isn't it wonderful? I thought he looked familiar, but he was just a little boy last time we saw him. I checked with Rosita, but when I went back to speak to him, he'd gone.'

She wasn't expecting Tom to look quite so angry about it.

'He's got a nerve,' he said. 'After the way that family treated poor Freda.'

'He was a little boy, Tom.'

'But he's been a man for a long time, Carol. He could have come back before now and just why has he come back, eh? Maybe he just wants to finish what his father started, had you thought of that?'

'Sorry I mentioned it,' Carol said.

'No, love, I'm sorry. Take no notice of me.'

'I won't,' Carol said and she went back, cupped his face in her hands and kissed him.

★ ★ ★

When Beth went down to open the shop her head felt sore to touch and she had a slight headache, but the headache was probably down to tossing and turning all night worrying about Lexi and trying to figure out exactly what she could do next.

It was raining heavily and the sea was a leaden grey beneath heavy purple-black clouds. She watched for a while, fascinated, as the rain left dents in the sand. The gulls were complaining noisily; at least, it sounded like complaining. For all Beth knew they might welcome the rain.

She checked her phone. No messages from Lexi. She sent her one anyway, then she sent one to Noah.

'Survived the night,' she wrote. 'Thanks for your help yesterday.'

He replied immediately.

'Glad to hear it. See you soon.'

A dog walker was her first customer, sitting at the table outside under the awning with his sandy, soggy black Labrador sitting at his side.

'You are serving coffee, aren't you?' he asked as Beth bent down to make a fuss of the dog.

'I certainly am,' she said. 'I haven't seen you before, have I?'

'Probably not.' He held out his hand. 'Rob Marsden. I don't walk Gemma on this beach while the summer people are here. I generally go over the nature reserve.'

'Beth Clarke,' she said. 'I'll get you that coffee. Would you like anything to eat? A cheese toastie or I could rustle up a bacon sandwich.'

'Go on, then,' he said, grinning. 'A bacon sandwich would go down a treat.'

'I'll just get a bowl of water for Gemma,' she said. 'She's beautiful.'

'She's smelly.' He laughed. 'I'll have to bath her when we get home.'

She made a sandwich for herself, too, and asked if he'd mind her joining him.

'I won't be offended if you say no. You obviously like some peace and quiet.'

'The company would be nice,' he said. 'I think you've already met my partner, Chloe. She runs the art gallery in town.'

'Yes, I did meet her,' Beth said remembering the petite blonde with the elfin haircut and huge blue eyes she'd met when she'd come for her last interview.

'I popped in earlier in the year and I've been meaning to go back. Perhaps now the summer season is over I'll have more time.'

'She'd like that.'

He saved a corner of his sandwich and gave it to Gemma who wolfed it down hungrily.

'You'd think she was starving, wouldn't

you?' He laughed. 'The vet's put her on a strict diet and it's not going down at all well with her. How much do I owe you?'

'It's on the house,' she said. 'As you're my first off-season customer.'

'Are you sure?'

'Absolutely. Besides, the bacon will go out of date tomorrow, so I have to use it up.'

'Tom would have a fit.' He laughed. 'But Carol would approve. She always said you had to have a big heart to live here. They both look so well since they retired. I think the job had got too much for them in recent years.'

'There is a lot to do. I was surprised quite how much.'

'They always seemed busy. Carol gave up working at the school so she'd be here all the time to help Tom. I suppose you know about that.'

'Yes,' Beth said. 'They seem a lovely couple, absolutely devoted to each other.'

''Morning!'

They turned to see Noah walking up the beach towards them, shoulders hunched against the rain, his hood pulled up.

'Time I wasn't here,' Rob said, getting to his feet. 'Don't tell Chloe about the bacon sandwich. I'm supposed to be watching my weight too.'

He patted his stomach. He didn't look overweight to Beth.

'I've put a bit on since I was made redundant so it's not just Gemma who's on a diet.'

He turned to Noah and his eyes narrowed for a moment, then he shook his head.

'I recommend the bacon sandwiches,' he said. 'Bye, Beth. See you again.'

'Would you like one?' she asked when Rob had gone.

'I'd love one, but I'd probably burst. You should have seen the size of the breakfast Rosita gave me this morning.'

'I know. I've stayed at the Lighthouse myself. How about a coffee, then?'

'I won't say no to that.'

He followed her inside.

'Was that Rob Marsden?'

'Yes, do you know him?'

'Used to. We used to go crabbing together when we were kids. I wish I'd realised before he left. It would have been good to say hello.'

'Never mind, I expect I'll see him around.' He looked thoughtful for a moment. 'I've got a list here as long as your arm,' he said. 'Someone told me you sell paint.'

'That's right. There are a couple of lockups in the car park. It's not a huge selection, but if you just want something neutral, it should be fine.'

'I won't want it just yet,' he said. 'I haven't been to Gran's yet so I've no idea what needs doing.

'I'm probably being optimistic thinking it'll just need a lick of paint after all these years. To be honest, I haven't told anyone else why I'm here.'

'So you're planning to stick around?'

'I've no plans to move on,' he said with a happy grin. 'It's about time I put down some roots and here seems as good a place as any. The happiest times of my life were spent at Furze Point. And to be honest, Beth, it was the thought of seeing you again that gave me the push I needed to come back.'

'Oh,' she said. 'Really?'

'Sorry. That makes me sound like some sort of mad stalker.'

'No, actually,' she took a deep breath, 'I've been hoping you would come back.'

Wow, did she really say that out loud? The smile he gave her turned her legs to jelly.

She rushed inside, made him a coffee, then sat down with him and he pushed a slightly soggy piece of paper towards her.

'I think I can help with most if not all of this,' she said as her eyes skimmed over the list.

'If you're planning on sleeping in a sleeping bag, I've got an inflatable mattress. You might find that more comfortable than sleeping on the floor.'

'Sounds great,' he said. 'Have you been up there at all? I was planning to go last night, but the light was running out and

I stopped by here. I'd already driven up earlier, but the road seems impassable.'

She looked blank.

'Your gran's house? I wouldn't know where that is.'

'Sorry, didn't I say? Most people call it Scott's Mansion. I used to address my letters to Laburnum Villa, Coast Road.'

Beth stared at him in shock. For some reason she expected his gran to live in a bungalow in town like Tom and Carol.

'Laburnum Villa? Is that what's it's called? You mean that mansion — the one up there?'

She waved her hand towards the beach houses, but knew the mansion was quite a distance beyond them.

'The big grand house with the stables?'

'It's not that big.' He laughed. 'And I doubt it's grand any more. Gran left it to me. She cut my mother out completely and my mother still refuses to talk about what happened between them.

'I don't know how people can do that, do you? Poor Gran.'

'It may not have been your mother's fault.'

'Not entirely. Six of one and half a dozen of the other! Isn't that usually the way? There's normally fault on both sides. Mum's just like Gran. Stubborn and feisty.'

'I haven't been up the road to the mansion, but Lexi went up there via the beach. She said some of the windows were broken.'

'Ah,' he said. 'I was afraid of that. That'll mean the weather has got in.'

'She said it's quite overgrown.'

'Well, it would be, after all this time.'

'What is it you do, Noah?' Beth asked. 'Apart from travel the world, I mean.'

'I'm a civil engineer, or I was,' he said. 'Not any more.'

'No?'

'I've got plans for this place,' he said.

'Right,' Beth said when he didn't elaborate. 'Let me see how much of this I can get for you.

'You're not going to be able to carry it all up to the mansion in one go, but I

114

can come along too and help with some of it.'

'I was hoping you'd say that,' he said. 'I can't wait to see it again and it would be great to have you along to share the moment.'

Shocking Discovery

The rain had stopped by the time they set off along the beach. The smell of the sea was stronger than she'd ever experienced.

'This is lovely,' Beth said. 'I haven't been further than the beach houses before.'

'Great, isn't it?' Noah said and he stopped for a moment, looking ahead to the muddy cliff where the roots of trees dangled down. 'I'm amazed those trees are still hanging on there, but perhaps they're not the same trees. We used to find fossils along this beach.'

As they started walking again, Beth was first to spot the boat moored in a creek.

'That's odd,' she said. 'Why would anyone leave a boat there?'

'I don't know,' Noah said. 'But the old boathouse is still there a bit further along the creek. See? Incredible.

'As far as I remember the creek goes

right through to the marshes. It's very deep at high tide, not worth trying to cross. If you do make it past, once you're past the creek and on to the marshes, it's a devil of a job to find your way back. The path up to the house must be close. I'm sure it's along here somewhere.'

He hurried ahead.

'Yes, here it is. Are you OK getting up or do you need a hand?'

'I'll be fine,' Beth said and they scrambled up a steep sandy path. Towards the end, Noah reached out his hand and held hers, helping her up the last few feet. She wondered if his skin tingled, too, where they touched.

At the top, they had to fight their way through a tangle of shrubs and brambles, but there was definitely an old path of sorts through there with light at the end.

'Someone's been through here recently,' Noah said, indicating the broken branches they passed. 'I doubt your sister did this. Mind the stinging nettles.'

Noah was in front and when they

117

reached the end, he stepped out into grass that was knee high. A path had been flattened, but he wasn't looking at that. Beth looked up and saw Laburnum Villa for the first time and when she glanced at Noah, she saw on his face the moment his heart broke and felt her own heart ache.

The beautiful house of her imagination and his memory was a wreck. Part of the roof was missing exposing the struts and they looked charred as if there'd been a fire. Most of the windows were smashed. The yellow bricks were grimy.

Without thinking, she reached out and touched his arm.

'I'm so sorry,' she whispered.

'The weather didn't do this.' He took a deep breath and turned to look at her. His eyes were cloudy. 'This is my fault. I should have come back years ago. I could have saved it.'

'You still can,' she said. 'It must be possible. If the structure is sound . . .'

'Who would do this?' he asked. 'What sort of person gets anything from destroying something like this?'

Beth thought of the homeless guy Lexi had told her about, but she dismissed the thought straight away. If he was living in the house, it wouldn't be in his interests to wreck it.

'I don't know, Noah. I used to see it where we used to live. A place would be abandoned and they'd have to put boards up at the windows. I know nature can cause some damage, but this was definitely people.'

He covered her hand with his and gave it a squeeze.

'Do you want to come in?' he said. 'I'd understand if you didn't.'

'Yes, I'll come in.' She wasn't going to let him do this alone. Goodness only knew what he'd find inside.

She felt angry on his behalf as they began to walk towards the house. Childhood was a safe place for many, somewhere they could revisit in their minds no matter what life threw at them.

Beth had precious memories of her own childhood before Dad died and she clung to them at times, drawing comfort from them. From what Noah had said, his happiest memories were here and seeing it like this could so easily tarnish them.

'They say you should never go back,' he murmured. 'Maybe I should have just sold this place and had done with it. My father wanted to buy it from me.'

'To live here?'

'No,' he scoffed, sounding bitter. 'It meant nothing to him. He wanted to tear it down and build houses on the site.' He reached into his pocket and pulled out a set of keys. 'Doesn't look as if I'll need these, does it?'

At the side of the house, a door had been forced open and was too damaged to close again.

'You don't have to come in,' Noah said again.

'I want to,' she said. The truth was she didn't want to leave him. 'You looked after me when I hit my head.'

'Which was my fault,' he smilingly reminded her. 'I don't need looking after, Beth, honestly. It's just been a bit of a shock that's all. You're welcome to come in if you want to, but I'd understand if you just wanted to get back to the Beach Hut.'

He pushed at the broken door and it opened enough to give them entry. The house seemed to be holding its breath as they entered. It smelled stale and sour, but there was something else. Food smells.

'Someone's living here,' Noah said, bristling.

'Wait. Lexi told me there's a homeless guy around. Maybe it's him. If it is, it doesn't mean he did the damage.'

'It's all right, Beth, I'm not going to go in all gung-ho and start throwing accusations around.'

They went into a huge entrance hall with a black and white tiled floor. Or at least it had once been black and white. It was impossible to tell what sort of state it was in beneath the dirt and broken glass. Noah let out a little groan.

'That was Gran's sitting-room,' he said as they moved towards an open door. 'My mother always called it the drawing-room.'

The door to the room was open and they approached slowly, broken glass crunching beneath their feet.

Rain had started to fall again, lashing against the windows as thunder began to growl in the distance. It seemed somehow appropriate.

'Good grief,' Noah whispered as they walked into the room. 'Why would anyone do this?'

Beth stopped dead, hardly able to believe what she was seeing. The room was a relic of an earlier time, but almost everything in it had been destroyed. A huge painting over the fireplace had been slashed and spray painted and there wasn't a wall that didn't have paint daubed all over it.

Sofas and chairs had been overturned and smashed. The carpet was stained and filthy. Even the curtains had been ripped from their hooks. Noah walked towards the piano which was still standing, but someone had gouged the wood.

He bent down and picked something up, brushing more glass to the floor as he straightened.

Beth hurried to his side and saw he was holding a framed photograph of a little boy standing next to a woman in a sunny garden. She was sitting on a chair, the kind they sold in the Beach Hut, her arms round the boy, her face bathed in happiness.

'You and your gran?' Beth asked softly.

'She was just . . . she was wonderful,' he said. 'My parents . . . they weren't cold exactly, but Gran made me feel special, as if I really mattered.

'I'd leave here and go back to school and my parents would be somewhere else in the world. I hated boarding school, but at least I could come here in the holidays and have some normality in my life until they decided to take me abroad with them.

'I knew it would be bad coming back. I didn't expect it still to be furnished, but to see it all destroyed like this is just heartbreaking.'

Beth put her arm round him.

'I'm so sorry,' she said. 'I don't know what to say.'

'It's not your fault,' he said. 'It's mine for expecting too much. I assumed my parents would have arranged to have the house cleared when they sorted out my ownership of it. I thought they'd at least make sure it was secure.'

'You can't secure anything against this sort of hateful vandalism,' Beth said, anger bubbling up inside her.

The fact that Noah was sad rather than angry made her even more furious. He seemed so nice and it was awful that people he didn't even know could hurt him like this.

A sudden thump from upstairs made them both look up at the ceiling.

'Someone's there,' Noah said. 'Stay down here, Beth.'

'Wait, Noah, don't go up there.'

He didn't have to. As they went back into the hall, a small group of people were coming down the stairs. Teenagers. The two boys looked like the pair Beth had seen walking along the beach before.

'Who are you?' one of the boys asked.

'More to the point, who are you?' Noah asked calmly. 'And what are you doing in my house?'

There were three girls with the boys and Beth felt a wave of nausea when she realised that Lexi was one of them, looking sullen and fed up, her hair dangling over her face.

'Lexi?' she gasped. 'What on earth are you doing here?'

'How did you find me?' Lexi said defensively.

'I wasn't looking for you,' Beth said. 'Are you responsible for this mess? The paint all over the walls? The damage?'

'We're just staying here, that's all,' Lexi said. She looked embarrassed.

'Staying here?' Beth snapped. 'In someone else's property when you have a perfectly good home to go to? How dare you, Lexi? I mean, really, how dare you? What's wrong with you? All of you! You should be ashamed.'

'Steady, Beth,' Noah murmured. He

was taking this a lot more calmly than she was. 'Don't say any more.'

'I want names,' Beth said. 'I'll be speaking to your parents, all of you! You should be thoroughly ashamed of yourselves.'

'Come on, let's go,' one of the boys said.

'You're not going anywhere.' Beth stepped in front of them and the boy who'd spoken squared up to her. He was much taller than her, but she wasn't going to back down.

'Let them go,' Noah said wearily. 'The damage has been done.'

'We didn't do this,' Lexi said. 'It was like this when we came here. How could you think I'd do something like this?'

'What's happened to you, Lexi? You're meant to be an adult and you're acting like a child. Why shouldn't I believe that you did all this damage? I don't even know you any more.'

Lexi came the rest of the way down the stairs. She was slightly taller than Beth and the look on her face made Beth

126

shudder.

'Acting like a child, am I? Well maybe it's because you've been treating me like one. Not once did you ask if I was OK with moving here. It's as if my opinion didn't matter to you at all. You went ahead and just arranged it without even discussing it with me. Have you any idea how much that hurt? I don't matter to you. In your eyes, I'm just a kid to be pushed around.'

'Hey, sorry,' the other boy said to Noah. 'We really didn't do this. We're from Stoursley and loads of people know about this place and come here. We just wanted to crash here for a few days.'

Noah nodded.

'Get out of here,' he said. 'Go on, the lot of you. You can put word round that the house is occupied now and anyone else found here will be dealt with by the police. Not you!' he added to Lexi. 'I think you should go home with your sister. You've a lot to talk about.'

'Noah,' Beth said, 'I can't tell you how sorry I am.'

'You go, too,' he said coldly. 'I'm going to start cleaning this up.'

'We can help,' she said. 'You don't have to do this on your own.'

'Yes,' he said, 'I do.' All the warmth and friendliness had gone from his eyes. He looked distant and hurt, but Beth longed to help him. 'I need to be on my own. Please, just go.'

'Noah . . .'

'I'll come back for the rest of my stuff later,' he said. 'Don't come back here, please, and for goodness' sake, talk to your sister.'

He turned away and she knew it was pointless trying to make amends. He was shocked and hurting and understandably so. He'd just found the happy place from his childhood in ruins, wrecked possibly beyond repair. He might be able to save the house, but what was inside it, the heart of it, was almost certainly gone.

Beth was so angry as she walked ahead of her sister back down the path to the beach. She didn't trust herself to say anything. The other kids were piling into the boat in the creek and setting off back to Stoursley.

'I suppose you want to go with them,' she said at last, her voice shaking. 'Your wonderful new friends.'

'They're not exactly friends,' Lexi shrugged. 'Just people I met.'

'But you thought you'd break into someone else's house and stay with them anyway? Tell me the truth, Lexi, were you responsible for any of that . . . ' she stumbled around for a suitable word. 'Artwork on those walls?'

'What do you take me for?'

'I don't know, Lexi.' She strode off again, wanting to put distance between them, but halfway back to the Beach Hut when she thought she had her anger under control, she turned back to look at Lexi. 'I don't think I know you at all. Where did you meet them?'

'Here,' Lexi said. 'They came over from Stoursley.'

'So you weren't even going round with anyone from the town? Why didn't you accept Adriana's friendship? She's a nice girl. Not like that lot.'

'No.' Lexi snorted as if such an idea was unthinkable. 'She's just a kid, still at school.'

'So were you until a few months ago.'

'You just don't get it, do you? The one thing you can't control is who I choose to be my friends. That is my choice, my decision.'

'I'll drive you back to uni,' Beth said, feeling defeated. 'I want you out of here as soon as possible so I can start trying to make things right with Noah.'

'No,' Lexi said. 'You won't drive me anywhere. I'm not going back.'

'What?'

'That's the end of it. I'm not talking about it any more. And that guy, Noah, it was him, wasn't it? The one that covered me in mud at the side of the road.'

'He warned you to keep out of the way.'

'What is he? Your boyfriend now?'

'Don't be ridiculous.'

'Yes, because that's all I am to you, isn't it? Ridiculous!'

Lexi took off down the beach at a run leaving Beth stunned. How had she turned it round so all this was her fault?

When she got back, Lexi was in her bedroom throwing her things in a bag. She didn't have much. Most of it was at the university, unless she'd already moved out. Tears were streaming down her face.

'Don't do this, Lexi,' Beth pleaded. 'Don't leave in anger like this. You know I love you.'

'Stop saying that. Actions speak louder than words, Beth, isn't that what you've always said? Well, why don't you think about your actions and see what they tell you.'

Beth winced. How had she managed to mess this up so completely? She'd handled it all wrong. Lexi was right, she should have taken her feelings into consideration instead of just expecting that she'd grow to accept everything.

'Where are you going to go? Lexi, wait, please . . .' She put out her hand, but Lexi shrugged it away. 'Just let me

131

know you're safe. Please.'

Lexi was breathing hard, her eyes fiery. She no longer looked like a child, but an angry young woman as she rubbed the tears from her face with the backs of her hands.

'I just need some space, Beth. Away from you.' She hauled her bag off the bed. 'Goodbye.'

Beth put out her hand.

'Remember I am always here for you.'

Lexi shrugged Beth's hand away and walked out. Beth followed her outside as she took the coastal path towards the town and she watched until Lexi was out of sight, then she went back inside the Beach Hut and sat down, burying her head in her hands.

She should have stopped her. She should never have let her walk out like that. But the only way would have been to physically restrain her and goodness knows how that might have ended up. All she could do now was wait and hope Lexi came to her senses and came home.

Broken Bonds

'Hello, Lexi, what are you doing here?' Carol heard Rosita ask and she dropped what she was doing and rushed out into the glare of the sun.

It had started off wet, but now there wasn't a cloud in the sky, but there was a chill in the air.

'Lexi! Aren't you supposed to be at university? Has something happened? Is Beth all right?'

At mention of her sister's name, Lexi's frown deepened.

'Oh, Beth is fine,' she said bitterly. 'Everything is right in her world.'

'But not yours, eh, love?' Carol said. She nodded at Rosita who moved away and carried on wiping down the tables.

'I have to get away from here,' Lexi said. 'Are there any buses? Or is there any way I can get a boat over to Stoursley so I can catch the train?'

'Can't Beth take you?'

Lexi's answering scowl told Carol all

she needed to know on that score. The sisters had clearly had a massive falling out.

'Why don't you sit down? I'll get you something to eat while I have a think. What do you fancy?'

'Could I just have a pastry and coffee?' Lexi asked. 'Please. Thank you, Carol.'

'You're welcome, love.'

Carol hurried back inside and Rosita followed her.

'What's going on?'

'I have no idea,' Carol said. 'But I'm playing for time at the moment. She looks as if she could use a shower. Do you think she's been sleeping rough? I think I'll give Beth a call. Don't let her leave.'

'I don't think she's going anywhere,' Rosita said, glancing out of the window where Lexi was wiping her eyes with her sleeve. 'What on earth is wrong there?'

'I wish I knew,' Carol said. 'I know Lexi didn't want to move here and that caused bad feeling between them. Beth raised her from when she was a little girl, so she's part parent, part sibling. It can't have been easy.'

'Lexi's an adult,' Rosita said. 'Old enough to know her own mind. When I was her age, I was married, expecting Adriana and buying a house. Perhaps Beth just hasn't realised Lexi has grown up.'

'I know, but look at her,' Carol said. 'She looks so lost and alone. They both seem such nice girls. Such a shame.'

Carol called Beth.

'Hello, Carol,' Beth said and Carol thought she sounded sad, there was no other word for it. 'What can I do for you?'

'I'm calling about Lexi,' Carol said.

'What about her?' Beth's voice hardened. 'What's she done now?'

'Done? She hasn't done anything. She's here at the Lighthouse asking if I know how she can get away from here.'

'It's probably for the best that she goes,' Beth said and Carol drew in her breath sharply.

'You don't mean that,' she said.

'I do,' Beth insisted, then her voice

135

broke and Carol suspected she was crying. 'No, I don't. I want her to come home, but that isn't going to happen, Carol.

'She hates me. I should never have made her come here. That doesn't excuse what she's done though. I'm still angry with her about that.'

It didn't sound as if Beth was going to rush down to the Lighthouse to see her sister and Carol wondered what terrible thing Lexi had done to make her sister so angry.

'I'm so worried about her, Carol. This behaviour is so out of character. I feel as if I don't know who she is any more and I just don't know what to do.'

'What did she do that was so awful?' Carol asked gently.

'Broke into Scott's Mansion for a start,' Beth said. 'Vandalised it, although she denies she had anything to do with it. You should see it, Carol. Such a mess. Poor Noah was devastated. I know he didn't expect the house to be in mint condition, but to find spray paint over

136

the walls and mindless destruction everywhere, it was just awful.'

'Noah?' Carol said feeling a thud in her chest. 'Noah was up at the mansion?'

'He looked so hurt,' Beth said. 'And so angry. But who wouldn't be?'

'And Lexi was responsible for all this damage?'

'She was with a group of kids,' Beth said. 'I don't know how much of it Lexi was responsible for, but she was there and she shouldn't have been.

'They said it wasn't them. Perhaps it wasn't. I don't know what to think any more, Carol. The Lexi I know would never have done anything like this.'

'I can try to keep her here until you can come over,' Carol said. 'You really need to talk about this.'

'I know, but she'll see me and run. I don't know what to do. I'm going to give her some space and time to think things through. I think we both need that. Right now I'm so disappointed in her and I'm even more disappointed in myself. I don't know what our parents would think about the way I've messed up.'

Carol bit her lip. She remembered how she felt when one of her boys took another boy's bike without permission. Oh, she always told herself that, but it was stealing, plain and simple.

Andrew, her youngest, had been fourteen at the time. Old enough to know better. He was very lucky that the other boy's parents didn't press charges and were happy with a proper apology from Andrew.

'Tell her to do whatever she has to do,' Beth said. 'She knows where I am if she needs me, but ask her to keep in touch. I need to know she's OK. Tell her I love her, Carol and if she wants to come back right now, I'd welcome her with open arms.'

Carol took a pastry and a coffee out to Lexi and sat down at the table with her.

'If you need a lift back to university, I'm sure Tom would take you,' she said.

'I'm not going back.'

'Oh, why not?'

'It wasn't for me, Carol. I didn't like it. I know Beth loved it for the short time she was there, but I felt out of place. I was doing it all to please her and in the end she threw it back in my face.'

'I'm sure she didn't mean it to seem like that,' Carol said.

'Perhaps not, but she did. Everything I did was to please Beth and she took my home away as if I didn't matter.' She looked at Carol, her eyes narrow with pain. 'It feels as if now I've turned eighteen, she no longer wants to know and at the same time, she still treats me like a child.'

'Even parents have to let go at some point,' Carol said gently. 'Letting go isn't the same as not caring. Beth is still young, too, and she's finding her way just as much as you are. So where will you go?'

'I don't know.' Lexi began to cry again. She looked so tired and that wouldn't help. 'I've made such a mess of everything and now Beth hates me.'

'She doesn't hate you.'

'You didn't see the way she looked at me at that big house. I honestly hadn't done anything except stay there. It was already falling apart and damaged. It hurts that she'd think I was capable of that.'

Carol put her arm round her.

'How about you come and stay with Tom and me for a while, just until you've got your head together and thought about what to do next?'

Lexi shook her head.

'I don't have any money. I can't expect you to keep me.'

There was no way Carol could leave this lost young soul to fend for herself.

'If you're certain you're not going back to uni, you could look for a job. If nothing else you could work for Fergus at Bluebell Farm. He often takes on casual workers. Or maybe you could help Tom in his new venture as a dog walker.'

Lexi picked up a paper napkin, blew her nose and wiped her eyes.

'Just temporarily.' She sniffed. 'I mean I don't want to stay here. That's what this was all about, remember. No offence, but I don't like it here.'

'None taken,' Carol said. 'My boys all moved away. The quiet life isn't for everyone.'

'Please, don't tell Beth I'm staying with you,' Lexi said.

'She'll want to know you're safe.'

'I'll text her every day. I don't want her to worry. I won't stay unless you promise not to tell her.'

Carol passed her another napkin and nodded. Lexi was clearly full of remorse and at least if she was staying with her, she'd know she was safe and could make sure she kept in touch with Beth.

'She asked me to tell you she loves you and if you go back, she'd welcome you with open arms.'

'You told her I was here? How do I know you won't tell her I'm staying with you?'

'You have to trust me, Lexi. Please.'

Lexi snorted. This was going to take time!

★ ★ ★

Beth was walking back from the car park a few days later when a tractor trundled towards her towing a trailer. She recognised Fergus from Bluebell Farm at the wheel. He was a big man, way over six feet tall and broad with it. Carol had described him as a gentle giant.

When he saw Beth, his ruddy face broke into a huge smile and he waved.

'The road up to Scott's Mansion is blocked, Fergus,' she called out. 'You won't get through.'

He stopped and turned the engine off.

'I know,' he said. 'That's where I'm going, to help Noah clear the road. We used to be friends when we were kids. There were three of us, like the three Musketeers.

'Tom used to take us crabbing in the summer holidays while Carol minded the shop. Sometimes Rob's dad would take us out in his boat proper fishing.'

'Sounds lovely, Fergus,' she said.

'It was like being part of a proper family, you know? I mean my dad tried his

142

best, but he was busy with the farm and didn't have time to do the usual father and son things.'

'Being a single parent can be hard,' Beth agreed.

'And Carol was like a mum to us all. And Mrs Scott was kind, too. It's hard to explain how it felt really, except I remember two childhoods, one with my dad and one with my other family.' He squeezed his eyebrows together. 'Does that make sense?'

'It does,' she said. 'In a strange way I feel as if Carol and Tom are my family, too, and I haven't known them as long as you.'

'That would make us honorary brother and sister.' He grinned. 'While I'm here with the tractor, if there's anything you need doing, let me know. You've got my mobile number, haven't you?'

Beth laughed.

'I do. Thank you, Fergus.' She had everyone's number. Her contacts list on her phone had never been so big. 'Actually, there is something you could do for me.'

'Name it,' he said.

'Noah bought a load of stuff, but he hasn't been back to pick it up. Would you be able to take it with you?'

She'd been hoping he would pop in to collect the rest of his purchases, but knew in her heart it was unlikely. She'd blown it with him. Or Lexi had, or else it was her reaction to Lexi being there.

Something had broken the connection they'd felt. She could have delivered the stuff, but he'd told her to go and said he needed to be alone.

'Sure,' Fergus said as he hopped down from his cab, surprisingly agile for such a big man. Beth wondered if Noah had told him what had happened at the house and how Lexi was involved.

She still burned with shame when she thought about it. And part of that shame was for how she'd reacted. She couldn't get the hurt look on Lexi's face out of her mind and as time passed, she realised she should never have jumped to conclusions.

At least her sister was texting every day to let her know she was all right which offered her some hope. Beth resisted the temptation to ask Lexi where she was and hoped eventually, when she was ready, that she'd tell her.

She helped Fergus carry the stuff to the tractor and loaded it into the trailer. There was a large shredding machine in the trailer.

'You're going to be busy,' she said and he ran his fingers through his untidy red hair.

'That's the plan,' he said. 'I've left someone looking after the farm so I can be here as long as Noah needs me.'

Bluebell Farm had been a dairy farm, but when Fergus took it over from his father, he'd retired the small dairy herd and turned his farm into a sanctuary where his girls, as he called them, could live out the rest of their lives in peace. Now he focused his efforts on growing and selling fruit and veg.

'If you fancy popping down to the Beach Hut later, I'm sure I can rustle you up something for lunch. Noah, too, if he'd like to come along.'

'Thank you, I'll tell him. I think we're going to be busy, though. Lots to do. I didn't think to bring anything to eat, to be honest, but I had a good breakfast.'

'OK. Well, the offer's open. Thanks for taking this for me, Fergus.'

He grinned.

'Any time, Beth.'

She wanted to say more, to give him a message for Noah, but what could she say?

Wasn't she always telling Lexi that actions speak louder than words? Fergus said he hadn't thought to bring lunch.

Smiling, she hurried back into the Beach Hut and got to work making a pack up. She'd take Noah and Fergus something to eat and a flask of coffee.

Just Like Old Times

Carol opened her front door to find a woman in her forties waiting outside. Her grey streaked hair was tied back in a ponytail and she was wearing an over-sized padded jacket and jeans.

'Rachel!' she cried. 'How lovely to see you. Come in, we're expecting you.'

'I'm a bit early,' Rachel said as she stepped inside and wiped her feet on the mat. 'Hi, you must be Lexi.'

'Hi,' Lexi said shyly.

'Tom told me you had a house guest,' Rachel went on. 'Is this one of your granddaughters, Carol?'

'Goodness, no,' Carol said. 'Lexi is a friend.'

'I see. I'm sorry I'm a bit early.' Rachel smiled awkwardly.

Carol had always been very fond of Rachel even though she seemed to get along much better with animals than people. She had hoped at one time that her eldest son, Paul would settle here with Rachel, but the lure of the city proved too much for him. It made her immensely sad that Rachel never seemed to find anyone else after Paul left.

'That's all right. It gives us time for a chat,' Carol said. 'I'll make coffee while we wait for Tom. He's just taking Freddy for a quick walk.'

'Freddy the Dachshund?' Rachel said. 'He was one of mine. Ex puppy-farm dog, poor thing, but he's had his happy ending with Miss Foster. Lovely lady. How is she?'

'She's been a bit poorly so Tom's been seeing to Freddy for her. So much for his dog-walking business. He's refusing to charge her anything because she's a friend.'

'Sorry to hear that she's not well,' Rachel said. 'But how typical of Tom not to charge. I hope no-one takes advantage of him.'

'He charges the people he knows can afford it,' Carol said. 'And it's worth it to them, plus it keeps him busy.'

'I'll make the coffee,' Lexi offered.

'Are you sure? Thank you,' Carol said, smiling. Lexi had proved to be such a perfect guest. She was quiet and helpful and Carol often got home to find the ironing done or dinner prepared. 'Shall we sit in the conservatory, Rachel?'

Once they were out of earshot and sitting down, Carol explained.

'Lexi is Beth's sister. I think Tom told you about our replacement at the Beach Hut, didn't he?'

'Yes, he did mention her. So why is she staying with you?'

'Long story. The girls had a bit of a falling out. Families, eh?' She could have bitten her own tongue. Rachel's rescues were the closest thing she had to a family since her dad died when she was in her twenties.

She'd been utterly devoted to him. It was no real surprise to anyone when she turned the house into an animal rescue.

She earned a living as a dog groomer and behaviourist which she could fit in around her rescue. She was also a qualified hydrotherapist and people came from miles away for her to help their pets recover from surgery and injury.

Just as Lexi brought their coffee in, Tom walked in the door.

'Rachel!' he said. 'Am I late?'

'No, I'm early,' Rachel said.

He turned to Lexi.

'Rachel was very nearly our daughter-in-law. She almost married our eldest son, Paul.'

Carol saw a flash of pain in Rachel's eyes and threw a look at Tom. He was a lovely man, would do anything for anyone, but he could put his foot in it at times.

Not that she was any better with her throwaway remark about families. Poor Rachel, she'd be wishing she hadn't bothered calling round.

'I understand you're interested in rehoming a dog,' Rachel said, getting down to business. 'I have one I think would suit you very well, but you'd need to meet her of course. Poppy is a German Shepherd.'

'I was hoping for something smaller,'

Carol said.

'Or more Labradory,' Tom added.

Rachel looked taken aback.

'I'm a rescue, not a breeder,' she said sharply.

'Oh, we know,' Carol said quickly. 'We didn't mean . . .'

'I think what Carol meant was, she's a bit worried about how she'd handle a bigger dog,' Lexi said. 'She'd want to be able to take her for walks and so on without worrying about being pulled over. And Tom — well, he's just Tom, isn't he?'

Now it was Tom's turn to look taken aback. Carol couldn't help laughing and Rachel joined in. With those few words, Lexi had changed everything.

'I would never suggest a dog that was likely to pull you over, Carol,' Rachel said. 'Poppy is very gentle and steady. She's not too keen on cats, but you don't have any other pets, do you?

'She's good with children of all ages and she's just a good all round dog. I do have smaller dogs, but they're very lively.

Poppy's owner passed away and she just wants a lap to rest her head on and a gentle hand to stroke her.'

She stood up to look out of the window.

'I see your garden is very secure — not that you'd need worry about Poppy trying to escape. She does have a long coat, though, so would require regular grooming, but I somehow think you wouldn't mind that. I remember the collie you had when . . .' she faltered.

She'd been about to say when she used to go out with Paul, Carol knew.

'Bess,' Carol said. 'She was a beautiful dog. You used to love brushing her for us, remember?'

'Yes, I remember,' Rachel said. 'Anyway, if you'd like to think about Poppy and come and see her, we can see if you take to each other. I do have other dogs, but I really think she'd be a perfect match for you.'

When they'd arranged to visit Poppy the following day, Carol saw Rachel out then returned to the conservatory, her face stony.

'Honestly, Tom,' she said, 'why do you have to mention Paul every time we see Rachel? The poor girl has never got over him.'

'But it's been years. They were just kids,' Tom protested.

'He was the love of her life and he broke her heart when he left,' Carol said. 'Men! Just don't mention Paul again. So, Lexi, are you going to come along with us to see Poppy?'

'I'd love to,' Lexi said. 'I love dogs. We couldn't have one in the flat, but Beth always said if we ever had a house . . .' She broke off and bit her lip. 'Too late now though, isn't it?'

'Have you texted her today to let her know you're all right?'

Lexi nodded.

'I do it every morning. I really should think about moving on, though,' she added. 'You've put up with me long enough. I can't stay here for ever.'

'There's no rush,' Carol said, patting her hand. 'You're welcome to stay here for as long as you like. We love having you, don't we, Tom?'

'Yes, yes, of course,' Tom said as the letterbox rattled. 'I'll get it.'

'Anything interesting?' Carol asked when he came back.

He shook his head.

'Just the usual rubbish,' he said. He looked quite shaken. Maybe Carol shouldn't have told him off quite so harshly about mentioning Paul.

* * *

Beth waited until lunchtime before setting off for Scott's Mansion and could hear the sound of the shredder working long before she came across Noah and Fergus at the top of the hill. They were both sweating despite the chill in the air, stripped down to T-shirts and jeans, but they'd made good progress.

Noah saw her first and stopped hauling branches about and stared at her. Fergus turned to see what he was looking at and gave her a cheery wave.

154

She hoped Noah would appreciate her peace offering. Things had been so going so well between them earlier and if he was to be a neighbour, she didn't want the atmosphere between them to stay sour.

She'd given up on her romantic hopes. Fergus flipped a switch and turned the shredder off and the silence was deafening.

'Thanks for sending my shopping with Fergus,' Noah said, but his voice was cool and clipped, and there was no hint of a smile. 'What can I do for you?'

'I just came to see how you were getting on,' she said cheerfully, even though she felt anything but. 'And I made you some lunch. I guessed you'd be working through and wouldn't have time to prepare anything.'

'That's very thoughtful of you,' Fergus said. 'Thanks, Beth.'

'Yeah, thank you,' Noah said with a flicker of a smile. 'You didn't have to do that.'

Oh, but I did, Beth thought. She had

such a lot of making up to do.

'It's just coffee and bacon sandwiches,' she said. 'And a couple of slices of quiche and some cake and crisps. There's a pot of potato salad, too, and some bread.'

'Is that all?' Noah said and she realised he was teasing. 'Sounds like quite a feast. Shall we take a break, Fergus? I hadn't realised how hungry I was.'

'Why don't you join us, Beth?' Fergus said.

'Oh, I don't want to intrude,' she said.

'Beth,' Noah said. 'It's fine. Really. I bet you haven't eaten.'

'Well, no . . .'

'Then join us,' he said. 'Please. I'm sorry for how I was the other day. I was shocked and upset and I took it out on you. It wasn't fair of me.'

'It was understandable,' she said, hope starting to rise again.

They sat down together on a fallen tree and she opened the cool bag.

'Sandwiches, quiche and potato salad are in there. I've got the cake and crisps in my backpack and a flask of coffee.'

'I'll just have some crisps,' Fergus said. 'And black coffee.'

'Oh. I made it with milk. I'm sorry, I didn't think.'

'No matter,' Fergus said. 'I've got a bottle of water in my cab.'

'But I made loads,' Beth said. 'More than enough.'

'Fergus, tell her,' Noah said with a chuckle.

'Tell me what?'

'I'm a vegan,' Fergus said and he looked down at the ground as if he was embarrassed.

'I'm so sorry, I didn't realise. I can nip back and make you something else.'

'No, really. I'm fine,' he said.

'Fergus was a vegetarian when we were kids,' Noah said. 'He used to get the mickey taken out of him something rotten.'

'The worst of it was my dad,' Fergus said. 'He took it as a personal affront that I wouldn't eat meat. Goodness knows what he'd think if he knew I'd given up dairy as well. He's probably rolling about

157

in his grave.'

'He'd be proud of you, Fergus,' Noah said. 'You're your own man doing what you believe to be right. No-one can knock you for that, but I'm sorry, those bacon sandwiches look too good to miss.'

He smiled at Beth as he took one.

'I was wondering if you needed any help with anything,' she said. 'Cleaning or painting. I'm pretty good at decorating and DIY and it's all quiet at the Beach Hut at the moment.'

'I haven't even started cleaning up yet,' Noah said. 'I've been going through Gran's things, sorting out what I can keep and what has to go.'

'All her stuff is still in there?' Fergus said. 'I had no idea. Everyone assumed the house had been cleared.'

'Well, it has, partially,' Noah said ruefully. 'All her jewellery has gone and anything of any value. A lot of the furniture is water damaged, but I'm sure there's a lot I can salvage. I think the fire that destroyed part of the roof may have been caused by a lightning strike and the rain put it out.'

'Your dad might have taken the jewellery,' Fergus said.

'My dad? But he hasn't been here.'

'Yes, he has. It was after Mrs Scott's funeral. Can't remember too much about it, but my dad said something about him wanting to sell the mansion and build houses in its place. People were talking about protesting, but he went away and never came back. I know he took boxes of stuff away with him. You're not going to pull the house down and build a housing estate are you, Noah?'

'No. I've plans for Laburnum Villa, but they don't include tearing the place down, not unless I really have to. Once the road is cleared I can get a surveyor in and find out the true extent of the damage.' His face broke into a smile that made Beth's heart skip a beat, but it wasn't for her. 'Well, hello, gorgeous!'

A black Labrador appeared at the bend in the road and bounded over to greet them, rudder of a tail going like the clappers as she went from one to another.

She spotted the sandwich in Noah's hand and sat down in front of him gazing up at him as if he was the only person on the planet.

'Gemma?' Beth said and the dog looked at her briefly and wagged her tail before turning her full attention back to Noah, or more particularly, his sandwich.

Moments later, Rob Marsden appeared, trotting up the road, out of breath and red in the face.

'There you are!' he said. 'Sorry about this. She can smell a picnic ten miles away. Fergus, Beth.' He nodded, then he looked at Noah.

'Good heavens, it's true then, you're back! I thought you looked familiar the other day outside the Beach Hut.' His face broke into a broad grin and held out his hand. 'How great is this? The old gang back together.'

'Even down to the black Labrador,' Noah said. 'Your Prince was always with us on our adventures. It's good to see you.'

Rob pulled Noah against him and the two men hugged.

'Beth's made us a feast. Why don't you join us?' Noah said, a smile in his voice.

'I'm tempted,' Rob said as he sat down on the fallen tree. 'I only had a lettuce leaf and half a tomato for my lunch. But I did run all the way up here chasing Gemma, so I probably burned off some calories. Go on then, you've twisted my arm.'

They all laughed as he helped himself to a sandwich and they began to talk about happy times way back in the past. Beth enjoyed listening to their stories, but she got to her feet and said she should be getting back.

'I'll drop all this in on my way back down the road,' Fergus said pointing at her bags. 'Thank you, Beth. You're a star.'

The others murmured agreement. There wasn't a lot of food left, but they hadn't started on the cake yet.

'Next time I'll be sure to include some vegan options for you, Fergus,' she said.

'You've gone all the way now then, Ferg?' Rob said. 'I'm not surprised. You always were soft over animals.'

Beth gave Gemma's head a stroke, then hurried back down towards the Beach Hut, arriving just as Carol was about to leave.

'There you are,' she said. 'I just wanted to check in, make sure you're OK. You are OK, aren't you, Beth?'

Carol looked a bit wary, Beth thought, as if she was holding something back. She shook her head, shaking the thought away.

'I'm fine,' she said. 'Have you time for a coffee? Lexi has been texting me every day. She seems to be getting her head together. I guess that's down to you.'

'Me?' Carol looked startled. 'Why me?'

'You passed my message on to her when you saw her at the Lighthouse. It obviously sunk in.'

'That's good,' Carol said and bit her lip. 'Were you up at Scott's Mansion?'

'Yes, they're clearing the road.'

'Noah's there?'

'Why don't you go on up? I'm sure he'd love to see you. He has nothing but happy memories of this place. If you hurry, they might even have some cake left to share with you.'

'They?'

'Fergus and Rob are up there, too.'

Carol looked thrilled.

'By the way,' she called over her shoulder as she walked away. 'We're getting a dog. We're going to take her for a walk tomorrow and if we all get along, we'll be bringing her home.'

'That's great news, Carol.'

★ ★ ★

Carol turned the corner and her heart jumped into her throat. It was like going back in time 20 odd years seeing the three boys sitting on the fallen tree, laughing and talking, especially with the black Labrador sitting in front of them.

They were all much bigger now of course, but still, she felt a warmth inside. She'd always thought of those three as her second family. Her boys had grown up and these three had filled a gap in their lives.

'Carol!' Fergus saw her first and waved. 'Come and join us!'

'Your knee giving you trouble?' Rob asked. She was limping a little. It had been quite a long walk uphill from the Beach Hut and she knew from experience that going downhill was often even more painful. There was no way she could even think of going back until she'd had a rest.

'Just a bit,' she said. 'But what about you, Noah Walsh?' she said. 'Why haven't you been to see us?'

He stood up, towering over her. It was hard to believe he was that same skinny little boy that used to wrap his arms round her waist and tell her he loved her. He was such an affectionate child. His grandmother, Freda Scott, had adored him.

It used to be so sad when his parents came to pick him up at the end of the summer. He always looked so small sitting in the back of their big car struggling not to cry.

'Big boys don't cry,' his father always said when Noah's chin started to wobble.

Now he hugged Carol and it was like being embraced by a bear.

'I'm sorry, Carol,' he said. 'I should have called in. I meant to. I didn't know where to find you.'

'Don't give me that,' she said tearfully. 'You only had to ask someone. And I work at the Lighthouse. I saw you having breakfast and thought I recognised you.'

'Why didn't you say hello?'

'I was going to after Rosita confirmed it was you, but when I came out to see you, you'd gone.'

'Well, here we are now,' Noah said. 'Sit down for a minute. Would you like anything to eat? There's not a lot left I'm afraid, but the cake is good.'

'I'm all right, thanks.'

Carol sat down and Gemma shuffled over and rested her head on her lap.

'So what have you been up to all these

years?' she asked as she stroked Gemma's soft head.

There was no more work done that day as the four of them sat talking non-stop. When it was time to go, Fergus helped Carol into his tractor cab. The tractor was an old one and Fergus's dad had had the small passenger seat put in for Fergus when he was a boy, but it was better than walking down the road. Carol had never sat in a tractor before.

'You look like an excited little girl,' Rob said.

'I feel like one.' Carol laughed. 'It's a shame I left my car in the car park. It would have been awesome to arrive home in this. That would make the neighbours look, wouldn't it! And Tom!'

'Don't be a stranger,' Noah said. 'You're welcome up here any time you like. We'll have the road cleared by the end of tomorrow so you can drive up. Bring Tom.'

She felt her smile falter, but waved cheerfully. At the moment bringing Tom wasn't an option. He seemed to have taken right against Noah and as far as she could see, it was for nothing he'd done.

'You should have a housewarming party, Carol,' Rob said. 'You cheated us out of giving you a retirement party and I really think we should mark the occasion in some way.'

The first thing that sprang into Carol's mind was the expense of such a thing.

'Oh, no, we couldn't possibly . . . '

But Rob had always liked his parties. He was always the one when they were children to suggest a barbecue on the beach or some such.

'Of course you could,' he said, warming to the idea even more. Noah and Fergus were nodding agreement. 'We'll all come and bring food and drink so you won't have to do anything. I'll get Chloe to make a cake. Got any plans for Saturday?'

'Well, no, but . . . '

'That's settled then. Shall we say seven?'

'No, really,' Carol said, trying to

167

sound firm. 'It's only a small bungalow. We can't host a party. Tom . . .'

'Would love it,' Rob said. 'And it'll all be friends. Go on, Carol, please. No beach house people, just friends and family. What do you say?'

Part of her reason for not wanting a big retirement party was the thought of inviting the beach house people. Nice as they were, they weren't all friends and some were quite aloof. But this would be different and if they all brought food, the expense shouldn't be too great.

And Rob was right, Tom would love it. No matter what he said, he missed being at the Beach Hut and seeing people all the time. No wonder he'd taken to dog walking.

'We might have our new dog by then,' she said. 'A party may frighten her. We're getting her from Rachel. She's a German Shepherd called Poppy.'

'Poppy?' Rob said. 'I remember her. Her owner died. I assumed she'd be taken in by one of his family. If I'd known, I'd have taken her myself. Lovely dog, and she gets along with Gemma, so I could bring her along, too. What do you think?'

Carol's resolve finally crumbled.

'The more the merrier,' she said. 'See you Saturday!'

Unwelcome Developments

Beth heard Fergus's tractor rumble past and smiled. He was such a nice guy, but wasn't everyone round here? She'd have no regrets at all about the move if it wasn't for the detrimental effect it had had on her relationship with her sister.

The tractor noise hadn't yet faded when there was a knock at the door and she was surprised to see Carol standing outside beaming all over her face.

'I had a lift in the tractor,' she said. 'It was awesome! And it saved my poor old knees. Mind you, they were poor knees even before I got old.'

'You're not old,' Beth said. 'Would you like to come in?'

'No, I shan't stay. Tom will wonder where I am. The boys want us to have a housewarming on Saturday and I wondered if you'd like to come?'

'Boys? Your sons?'

'Our honorary sons,' Carol said. 'Fergus, Noah and Rob, but we could invite our sons and their families over. I doubt they can come at such short notice, but you never know. You will come, won't you, Beth?'

Beth hesitated. Noah had been friendly enough earlier, but would he want her around at a party?

'Please say yes,' Carol said. 'I might have a surprise for you.'

'A surprise? Sounds intriguing. What can I bring?' Beth asked.

'Whatever you like, my lovely,' Carol said. 'I think Chloe is making a cake. It's a bit late having a housewarming so long after we moved in, but never mind. I just hope Tom will come round to the idea.

'Noah isn't his favourite person at the moment, but it's not Noah's fault. He's done absolutely nothing wrong. It was his parents really that upset Tom. Anyway, I'm rambling. I'd better go.'

She moved forward and gave Beth a hug. Beth hugged her back. It was really strange. Until she moved here, she rarely hugged anyone, but now it was coming as second nature to her.

Even Lexi, close as they were, didn't hug a lot. The only time was if Lexi was upset about something, until recently anyway. Now if Lexi was upset she was more likely to push Beth away. If only she hadn't run off like that. If only I hadn't let her, Beth thought.

But she couldn't have stopped her. If there was one thing Lexi was, it was determined. She'd seemed so determined to do well in her A-levels and get into a good university, but it had all just fallen apart so suddenly.

Why had she changed her mind about her future? Or had she just been trying to please Beth by doing well at school? She bit her lip.

Some time after Carol had gone, Beth was sitting by the window in the dark watching the moon dip in and out of the clouds. One minute the sea was sparkling in the moonlight and the next it was invisible in the darkness. The outlook here was ever changing and she marvelled that a flat expanse of sea could look so different from one day to the next, one hour to the next, even.

She heard the sound of voices down on the beach and as the moon cast beams of light across the sand she saw a group of people coming her way from the direction of the beach houses.

Beth remembered what Lexi had said to her about making sure she kept her doors locked, then told herself she was being silly. They were probably just some youngsters out for a walk in the moonlight. But the doors were locked anyway. She always made sure of it.

The beach and sea darkened as clouds completely obscured the moon and when they cleared again, the beach was empty.

Then Beth heard the door downstairs rattling and nearly jumped out of her skin.

She leapt to her feet, almost knocking the table over in her hurry to turn the lights on so that light would spill from the windows upstairs across the sand. Her heart was thumping. The rattling continued for a moment, then she heard a shout and cupped her hands against the window in time to see four people running across the sand back towards the beach houses.

What if they were planning to try the doors of the beach houses? She grabbed her jacket and a torch and hurried downstairs, locking the door behind her.

She could see them prancing about further along the beach and called out.

'What are you doing here?'

They said something she couldn't hear and there was laughter.

'Lexi?'

It was a horrible feeling, thinking that they might be up to no good and that Lexi might be with them. She was sure they were the ones that had been in Noah's house.

Some of the beach houses had CCTV and she'd be checking that in the morning, but for now, she just wanted them gone.

'Wait!' she called as they started to run down the beach away from her. She chased them for a while, but there was too much distance and it was hard running on the soft sand.

She ran to the end of the beach houses, then worked her way back, checking them one by one, making sure no doors had been forced or windows broken, although the windows were double glazed and breaking them would be difficult.

By the time she was halfway along, she heard the chug of an outboard motor and looked out to see a boat heading past, no doubt on its way back to Stoursley, or even the other side of Furze Point.

They must have been moored in the creek near the mansion. She wondered if they'd been bothering Noah and hoped he was all right and had managed by now to make the house secure.

Going up and down the steps to the beach houses was tiring. No wonder Carol had ended up with bad knees. She'd only had a few houses left to do when she heard a shout and froze, seeing someone heading towards her. Perhaps they hadn't all gone after all.

'Wait there! Don't move!'

It was a man's voice and he sounded

angry, but he couldn't be as angry as Beth was right now. These people could cost her her job and her home if they damaged any of the beach houses.

'No, you wait there!' she shouted back. 'Don't you move!'

She ran down the steps and her foot slipped sending her sliding all the way down on her back, yelping all the way. Oh, for goodness' sake! How was she supposed to sound authoritative and intimidating when she couldn't even manage a few steps without falling over her own feet?

The guy was running towards her and she struggled to get up, ready to defend herself. There wasn't a bit of her that didn't hurt and she didn't know what she was going to do, but she was determined to put up a fight.

'Beth? What were you doing up there?'

'Noah? I thought you were one of that gang of kids. I assume they were kids.'

The enormity of it all hit her like a sledgehammer and she sank back on to the bottom step. What had she been thinking, chasing after them like that? What if it had been one of them coming back?

'Have they done anything?' he asked, looking up at the house. 'I thought you were an intruder when I saw you.'

'Not that I've found. I've just got a couple more to check,' she said and her voice shook.

'Here,' he said, holding out his hand. She hesitated for a second before reaching up and staggering slightly.

'Are you all right?'

'I'm fine,' she lied. No need to tell him about the pain which stretched from her shoulders down to her knees. She must have hit every step on her way down.

'It was quite a fall you took.'

He must think her very accident prone.

'My fault for rushing,' she said.

'What were you going to do?' he asked and although she couldn't see his face, she could hear that he was smiling.

'I'd have figured that out when I caught you,' she said.

'Seriously though, you shouldn't be

chasing people down the beach in the dark. I know they shouldn't have been here, but if you were worried you should have called the police. Or me! You still have my number, don't you?'

It hadn't even occurred to her to call him. Why would it?

'Did you see them? Was Lexi with them?' He sighed.

'I don't think so. Look, you have to stop thinking the worst of your sister. She said she wasn't responsible for what happened and I believe her. You should, too.'

'Whether she was or not, she shouldn't have been in your house.'

'What kid hasn't been in an apparently abandoned building?' he asked.

'She's not a kid. She's an adult and should know better.'

'You're still mad at her. How is she?'

'I don't know,' Beth mumbled. 'She's gone. She's still in contact with me, but she says she's not going back to uni.'

Feeling thoroughly told off, she started to walk towards the next of the beach houses, but the pain made her limp.

'You are hurt,' he said.

'I'm fine.'

'And stubborn. Why won't you accept help when it's offered? I'll check the rest of the houses. You should sit down for a minute and get your breath back.'

The houses had to be checked and she couldn't see herself getting up and down several more flights of steps so she nodded.

'Thank you.'

'It's what friends are for,' he said as he helped her back to the steps so she could sit down. 'And we're neighbours, too. Next-door neighbours if you disregard the beach houses. Stay there. I won't be a minute.'

That was all she was to him now, a neighbour. Not that she'd ever been anything else. Perhaps she'd imagined the closeness between them. He'd said it was the thought of seeing her again that lured him back, but was it true? Maybe he was just teasing her.

She watched the torch beam and listened to his footsteps going up and down the wooden steps until he'd reached the house at the end.

One thing was for sure, she thought as she pulled herself painfully to her feet, this was going to hurt tomorrow.

'Everything looks fine,' he said as he came back. 'Now we need to sort you out. I'll drive you to the hospital.'

'No,' she said. 'There's no need.'

'You should be checked out.'

'There's only a minor injuries department and it closes at five,' she said. 'And I certainly don't want to go miles to the nearest town only to be told what I already know. I'm bruised, that's all.'

'You didn't hit your head?'

'No.'

'Sure about that?'

'I don't make a habit of going round bashing myself on the head,' she said.

'I'm sorry, Beth. You must wish you'd never set eyes on me. I seem to have brought you nothing but back luck.'

'I wouldn't say that,' she said. 'You pulled us out of the ditch that day.'

'And covered your sister in mud,' he

said. 'Which I don't think helped sisterly relations. Come on, I'll walk you home.'

'I'm fine.'

'Yes, you probably are, but I'll still walk with you if you don't mind.'

She tried her best not to limp as they walked along the beach to the Beach Hut.

'You can hold on to my arm if you like,' he said and she was going to turn him down, but pushed back her stupid pride and slid her arm through his. It didn't take the pain away, but it made her feel a lot better.

The lights were still blazing out from the flat.

'They were trying to get in,' she said. 'I turned all the lights on which seemed to scare them off.'

'I think they were looking round my house, too,' he said. 'I definitely heard something and I thought of you on your own down here. That's why I came to check you out. But they've gone now. I saw them going out in their boat.

'I'll ask around, see if anyone knows

who they are. It might be it just needs a word from their parents and this will stop. I'll come inside to check the place out if you'd like.'

She remembered Lexi's warning. Did she know her so-called friends were planning this?

'I don't want to put you out, Noah,' she said. 'You've already done so much.'

She would like him to check the Beach Hut. Even though she'd locked up, there was still a niggle of fear worrying away at her. What if someone had got in?

'Put it another way. I'd feel better if I checked it out,' he said. 'But first I'd like to buy something from the shop.'

'What do you need?'

'I'll know it when I see it,' he said with a grin. Inside, he went round the shop then headed towards the first aid shelf and picked up a large bottle. 'Ah ha! Here we are.'

'Witch hazel?'

'It was Carol's go-to remedy for every-thing from bruises to insect bites. She used to say it'd bring the bruise out and make it less painful and take the swelling out of bites. I don't know how true it is, but I used to like the smell and I always felt better after having some dabbed on with cotton wool. Put it in the fridge then after you've had a bath or shower, dab some on. If you can.'

'I'll try anything,' she said.

'Arnica is good for bruises, too, but I bet you don't stock it.'

'Probably not.' Beth looked round the store. Something had been niggling at her since she took over and now she knew it was time she did something about it. The whole place needed updating. They had things on the shelves that no-one would ever buy.

'Thanks for your help,' she said. 'Again.'

'You're more than welcome. If anything like this happens again, give me a call. I can be here pretty quickly. Are you going to Carol's party on Saturday?'

'I think so.'

'We could go together, if you'd like. That way there won't be too many cars looking for spaces round there. I'll pick you up on my way past.'

'Thank you, that would be great.' She was more pleased than she ought to be that he was giving her a lift.

She'd never met anyone quite like Noah before. He seemed such a gentle person and yet he made her feel safe. When he'd been shouting at her on the beach, thinking she was an intruder, he'd sounded quite scary!

He checked round the Beach Hut, then waited until she'd locked the door behind him before setting off back along the beach at a jog.

Smiling, Beth leaned against the bolted door and winced in pain, her smile vanishing. Painkillers and a hot shower were needed, then off to bed.

Back at Laburnum Villa, Noah's brain was buzzing. He knew he'd never get to sleep despite being physically tired and he took his most powerful torch through to his gran's bedroom.

He hadn't even started on that room yet and even in the dark it still looked painfully familiar.

He could remember climbing into that bed with her and curling up beside her when there was a thunderstorm.

She'd put her arm around him and tell him stories doing all the different voices until he relaxed. He'd still jump with every crash of thunder, but he felt safe in her arms.

In the corner of the room stood her bureau. She had a study downstairs, but used to prefer to sit up here to write her letters and pay her bills. At some point, someone had rifled through it and he started to gather up papers and letters from the floor.

He found a letter written by his eleven-year-old self, telling her about his new home. In places the ink was blurred and he'd drawn an arrow pointing to the patches.

'My tears,' he'd written in the margin. He felt tears gather in his eyes now, remembering how lonely he'd been and how much he missed Freda. She must have been so upset to receive his self-pitying letters.

I could at least have put on a brave face, he admonished himself silently.

He found a large manilla envelope and recognised his father's writing.

Inside was a set of detailed plans for what looked like a housing estate. Notes said how much it would cost to clear the lane, chopping down trees and levelling it all, turning it into a proper access road.

It had all been professionally put together and was dated prior to Freda's death. Was that the reason for their falling out? Gran would have fought tooth and nail against selling her mansion and all the land. It had been built by her grandfather and meant the world to her.

'It'll be yours one day,' she used to tell Noah. Maybe that was why. She knew what plans his parents had for it, knew they wouldn't love it the way she had.

Without thinking, he wrestled his phone from his pocket and called his mother.

She took ages to answer and when she did, her voice was muffled and heavy with sleep.

'Noah?' she said. 'What is it? It's . . . ' she was clearly fumbling for the time. 'Four in the morning! Are you in trouble?'

He gave a short, bitter laugh. That was typical of his parents, always thinking the worst of him. He realised that was why he had cooled so much towards Beth, the way she'd assumed her sister was responsible for the mess.

It was very unfair of him. Their situation was entirely different.

'Noah?'

'Mum,' he said. 'Did you and Dad try to persuade Gran to sell the mansion?'

'What? You call me up in the middle of the night to ask me that?'

'Sorry,' he mumbled. 'I forgot about the time difference. But it's important.'

'Well, yes, we did. Your dad had the plans drawn up — at considerable expense to us, I might add. If she'd agreed, that place would have been worth a small fortune. Why?'

'Just wondering,' he said. 'And after Gran died . . . Did you go to the funeral?'

'We couldn't get back in time.'

He heard his father's voice in the background.

'It's Noah,' his mother said.

'What does he want? Let me talk to him.'

Noah sighed.

'Dad. I'm at Laburnum Villa.'

'At last,' his dad said. 'I've wanted to talk to you about that place for years. So you've finally seen sense. I can get a flight over and we can discuss what to do with it.'

Noah closed his eyes. He hadn't seen his parents for months. The truth was, they'd never been all that interested in him.

'No, Dad,' he said. 'I have plans of my own.'

'Well, that's good. Call me tomorrow and we'll talk.'

'OK. Sorry I disturbed you.'

He shone the torch over the plans.

No wonder Freda Scott had fallen out with her daughter and son-in-law if this was what they'd wanted to do to her beloved home.

The Party's Over

'She's beautiful,' Carol said as soon as she laid eyes on Poppy. The Shepherd was mostly black with tan stockings and when she heard Carol's voice, her big brush of a tail began to wag.

'Take her for a walk,' Rachel said, handing Carol the lead. 'See how you get along.' She looked at Lexi. 'Nice to see you again, Lexi.'

Lexi smiled.

'It must be wonderful doing this,' she said. 'I'd love to work with animals.'

'It is wonderful, but it can be heart-breaking,' Rachel said. 'I can always use an extra pair of hands if you have any free time. I can't afford to pay much, I'm afraid. I'm going out later to try to trap a cat and her kittens. You're welcome to come along.'

Lexi looked at Carol and she laughed.

'You don't have to ask my permission, lovely,' she said. 'Are you coming for a walk with us?'

'Is it all right if I wait here with Rachel?' Lexi asked.

'Of course.'

Carol smiled to herself. Of all the unlikely friendships! Lexi had been introduced to all sorts of people, but she seemed to have struck up a rapport with Rachel who was more than 25 years her senior.

Carol slipped her arm through Tom's and they walked down the lane beside Tiny Tails with Poppy trotting along beside them.

'She's younger than I thought,' Carol said. 'I was expecting an older dog.'

'Me, too,' Tom said. 'She's lovely, though, isn't she? So beautifully trained and so calm.'

He seemed to be in such a mellow mood which was rather different from how he'd been for the past couple of days. Carol hadn't had chance yet to speak to him about the party on Saturday. Walking down this quiet lane bathed in soft yellow sunlight, it seemed the perfect moment.

'Party?' he said looking pleased. 'Really?'

'And we don't have to do anything. Our guests are going to bring food and drink. You could fire up the barbecue if it's fine and do some sausages.'

'Whose idea was this?'

'It was the boys,' Carol said. 'Our honorary sons.'

'Fergus and Rob,' Tom said looking even more delighted.

'And Noah.'

His smile vanished.

'Surely he's not coming.'

'Surely he is,' Carol said adamantly. 'You can't hold a grudge against him for what his parents did or didn't do. Paul is going to come and Simon says he'll try. Andrew's got other plans. Paul says he's going to make a weekend of it and stay over with us.'

'That's great,' Tom said, 'but don't expect me to act as if nothing happened as far as Noah is concerned.'

'Oh, Tom, if you'd seen Noah. He's still the sweet person he always was. Remember how protective he was over

Fergus, our gentle giant?'

'He could have kept in touch,' Tom said.

Carol felt a tug on the lead and realised Poppy was watching them, concern in her eyes.

'Tom,' she said, 'let's not argue in front of Poppy. She won't want to come and live with a pair of old grumps.'

'Sorry, girl,' Tom said, bending over to fondle Poppy's soft head and the dog seemed to smile up at him, reassured.

'OK. I'll behave at the party, but I won't be welcoming Noah with open arms. I was hurt when he lost touch. I thought we meant something to him and then when none of them turned up for Freda's funeral, but his father managed to come here afterwards, it was just the last straw.'

'He was a child,' Carol said. This was so unlike Tom. He always used to be the most easy-going man and he loved spending time with the boys. He should have been as thrilled as she was that Noah was back. She hoped that once he saw him that all that resentment would melt away.

★ ★ ★

When Beth and Noah arrived at the party, the bungalow was heaving with people. Fortunately it was a mild evening and several people were out in the garden.

Noah had brought flowers, wine and beer and Beth had made a large quiche and walnut muffins, with Fergus in mind.

The dining table groaned under the weight of all the food, loaded with everything from Fergus's delicious looking salads to Rosita's huge scones.

'You're here,' Carol cried, rushing towards them and hugging them each in turn. 'I'm sure you know everyone, but there's someone rather special I'd like you to meet.' She grasped Beth's hand just as a tall man with greying hair was passing.

'This is my son, Paul,' Carol said. 'Paul, this is Beth.'

He shook Beth's hand and smiled.

'Pleased to meet you, Beth. Hope you've settled in OK. Mum and Dad have talked non-stop about you.'

'That's enough of that,' Carol said and continued to lead Beth through the crowded living-room.

Beth cast a glance over her shoulder at Noah and the smile he gave her made her stomach turn over. It was silly to even let herself entertain such thoughts about him. He was just a nice guy who was being neighbourly that was all, but the way he looked at her sometimes told a different story.

'Are you all right, Beth?' Carol frowned.

'A bit stiff,' Beth said. 'Nothing to worry about.' No need to tell anyone about her tumble down the steps and the fact she was well dosed up on pain-killers, especially not Carol who would only worry.

'Is this your surprise?' Beth said when a beautiful near black German Shepherd ambled over to say hello. 'Isn't she beautiful? Is she yours? The dog you were telling me about?'

'She certainly is,' Carol said. 'She settled in immediately. We took her for a walk, then when we got back to Rachel's, instead of going inside, she went to stand by our car.'

'How wonderful,' Beth said. 'I'm thinking of getting a dog myself. Perhaps I can speak to Rachel about it some time.'

She hadn't realised quite how isolated she would feel living in the Beach Hut off season and a dog would be a welcome companion. And what a lovely life she could give a dog at their home on the beach.

'You should speak to Rachel,' Carol said. 'She's around somewhere. Let's try to find her.'

Beth looked behind again and saw Noah still trying to follow, but being stopped every now and then. It seemed everyone wanted to say hello to him. He was like the town's very own prodigal son. He threw her an apologetic look and she smiled ruefully, her heart jumping.

'She must be out in the garden,' Carol said as Beth said hello to Rosita and Chloe. Gemma was there too and Beth stopped to say hello to the Labrador before following Carol outside.

More people were gathered in the garden where someone had strung strands of colourful lights and Tom was standing behind his barbecue chatting to a couple of men. Beth looked at Carol and she gave a happy little laugh.

'Over there,' she said.

What was this about? Beth followed Carol's gaze and saw a woman with a grey ponytail. She was talking to someone Beth couldn't see, but then she moved to one side and her eyes met Lexi's.

Her heart thumped.

'What's she doing here?' she said.

'She's been staying with us, Beth,' Carol said.

Lexi's face registered shock, then she scowled as she came towards them.

'You didn't tell me Beth was coming,' she said and Beth winced. 'I trusted you, Carol.'

'She's been staying here and you didn't think to tell me, Carol?' Beth said. 'Don't you think that's a bit underhand?'

'I was giving you both time to cool off,' Carol said. 'Now you're here, for goodness sake talk to each other. I'll get you a drink.'

Carol hurried away.

'Beth, I . . .'

'Lexi . . .'

They laughed.

'Go on,' Beth said. 'You first.'

'I was going to say I'm sorry,' Lexi said. 'This place isn't so bad and you were right about the people being friendly. Carol and Tom have been so kind. I made Carol promise not to tell you I was here. I said I wouldn't stay if she told you.'

'I see. Do you think you might come h— back to the Beach Hut?' Beth asked, correcting herself just in time.

'Do you know why I was so upset? Do you understand yet?'

'You didn't want to move here,' Beth said. 'I get it.'

'No,' Lexi said. 'You don't. All my

life I've tried to please you. I was going to university because that's what you wanted. I put my life to one side so I'd get the A-level results I needed and I saved every penny from my Saturday job.'

Beth felt the sting of tears. Suddenly Lexi sounded exactly what she was, a young woman and not a stroppy teenager with a huge chip on her shoulder.

'Then out of the blue you announced that we were leaving to live here. Not once did you ask for my opinion. You just went ahead and accepted the job and gave up our flat and all our furniture and it was as if my opinion didn't matter.'

'I had no choice.'

'Beth! Maybe you had no choice about moving here, but you didn't have to shut me out of it,' she said.

'I don't think I'd have objected, but I felt so hurt, so side-lined. It was as if once I was going to university, you'd washed your hands of me. Why did you do that?'

'I don't know,' Beth said truthfully.

'I thought there was no choice and the decision had to be taken, but I see it now. I should have involved you. I was wrong and I'm sorry. Do you really not want to carry on at university?'

'No, I don't. I was doing it for you, Beth, and that's not a good reason to do something. I'm sorry about what happened at the mansion, too. It was stupid. I should never have gone there. It felt wrong at the time, but I was so angry.'

Noah came over with two glasses.

'Carol sent these,' he said. 'Hi, Lexi.'

His smile, Beth noted, was genuine. He really didn't hold it against Lexi that she'd been in his house with her friends.

Noah felt a hand on his shoulder and turned to see Tom.

'So you came back,' Tom said quietly. 'Come and talk to me. I can't leave the barbecue unattended.'

Noah cast an apologetic glance at Beth and followed the older man to the other side of the garden.

'It's good to see you again, Tom,' Noah said.

'Is it? Is it really?' Tom said stiffly. 'Why have you come back?'

'I have plans for Laburnum Villa,' Noah said and he couldn't disguise the excitement in his voice.

'Huh,' Tom growled. 'Would these be the same plans your parents had?'

'I didn't know they had plans,' Noah said. 'Until last night. I found them in Gran's bedroom.'

'She should have burned them,' Tom said vehemently. 'She showed them to me and asked if I thought she was a selfish old woman for wanting to keep the mansion as it was. Your parents made her feel like that.'

'Poor Gran.'

'She was heartbroken, mainly because they'd fallen out which meant she no longer saw you. She adored you.'

'She never told me any of that, in her letters, I mean,' Noah said. 'I had no idea. I didn't even know she'd died until years after. My parents let me think she'd lost interest in me.'

Tom snorted.

'And you believed that?'

'I got in trouble at school,' Noah said. 'It wasn't anything massive, but my parents said I'd brought shame on the family and Gran would be heartbroken about it.

'I begged them not to tell her. I think I'd hoped that if I was bad, I'd be sent home to Gran. What an idiot.'

Noah stopped talking. He hadn't told anyone else this and now he was opening his heart to a man who couldn't have been less pleased to see him.

'You were a child,' Tom said.

'I assumed they told her. I assumed she was ashamed of me. I assumed too much instead of searching for the truth and when I did, it was too late.'

'Your father turned up here after the funeral with his lawyer. He wanted to overturn Freda's will and tried to say she wasn't in her right mind when she left it all to you.

'He was still waving his copy of those plans about, insisting a new housing estate on the land would be good for the town.'

'I hope you all ran him out of town,' Noah said softly and to his surprise, Tom laughed.

'Not quite, but as good as. We left him in no doubt he wasn't welcome here, then we waited for you to come back once you were old enough. And you never did.'

'Until now,' Noah said.

'Dad!' Paul stood at the back door. 'Dad! There's someone at the front door to see you. They're not here for the party.'

'I'll take over,' Noah said. Tom looked at him for a moment, then nodded and handed him the barbecue tongs.

There was something strange in the air. Beth felt a shift in the atmosphere as Tom hurried down the side of the bungalow.

'What's going on?' Lexi said.

Beth looked round. Noah was at the barbecue chatting to someone. It all seemed so normal and yet something felt wrong.

'I don't know. Who is the woman you were talking to? She seems to be on her own. Would you like to introduce us?'

'It's Rachel,' Lexi said and to Beth's surprise, she took her arm and led her across the garden.

'Rachel runs Tiny Tails, the rescue place. I've been helping her out. She can't pay me much, but at least I feel I'm doing something useful until I can get a paying job. Rachel, this is my sister, Beth.'

Here? Beth wondered. Was Lexi looking for a job here? Dare she let herself hope?

'From the Beach Hut?' Rachel said, her face breaking into a smile. She wasn't wearing make-up, but was quite stunning to look at with her large grey eyes and warm smile. 'It's so lovely to meet you. I've heard such a lot about you.'

'It's good to meet you, too,' Beth said. 'Actually, I was hoping to speak to you at some point. I'm thinking of getting a dog.'

'You've come to the right person,' Rachel said. 'Why don't you come over with Lexi on Monday and we'll have a proper chat?'

'I'm going there about ten o'clock,' Lexi said. 'You can come and pick me up if you like.'

'I would like,' Beth said, her heart full. 'Very much.'

Music had been playing, but it suddenly stopped and everyone fell silent as Tom came back. He walked over to the barbecue and took the tongs out of Noah's hands.

'I'm sorry, everyone,' he said. 'The party's over.'

'What? Tom!' Carol cried.

'I mean it,' Tom said. 'I think you should all leave now. You can take your food with you if you want. I'm really sorry, but . . . ' He looked around. 'It's finished.'

'Tom! You can't send people away. We're only just getting started. Please, everyone, don't go . . . ' She turned to the guests who were already starting to leave. 'He didn't mean it.'

'Dad?' Paul said. 'What's going on?'

'I just want them all to go,' Tom insisted

and his voice cracked. 'Get them out of here. Now, Paul. Please.'

Carol rushed round apologising as everyone left. She clutched Beth's hands.

'Thank you for coming. I'm so sorry. I don't know what's got into him.'

'You should go, too,' Tom said to Lexi. 'Take her home with you, Beth. Get her away from here.'

'Have I done something wrong?' Lexi asked. She sounded so upset, so broken, that Beth's heart ached for her.

'Grab what you need,' Beth said. 'We can come back for the rest of your stuff another day. Carol, are you going to be OK?'

'Yes . . . no . . . I don't know. Paul is here.'

Her son came over and put his arm round her shoulders.

'It'll be all right, Mum. We'll sort this out. I'm so sorry, Beth. It was nice to meet you. And you, Lexi.'

'Lexi hasn't done anything wrong,' Tom muttered. 'I just need it to be close family here tonight.'

Lexi went to her room and grabbed her stuff.

'I've got everything,' she said. 'I didn't have much.' She wrapped her arms round Carol. 'Thank you for everything you've done for me. You have my number if you need me. Let me know you're all right, please.'

'I will, lovely,' Carol said. 'Thank you for being such a perfect house guest. Look after her, Beth. She's a good girl, really she is.'

'I know,' Beth said.

Carol began to cry as Tom ushered the last of their bemused guests out of the door.

'I'll look after her,' Paul said. 'I'm not leaving until this is all sorted out.'

Noah stopped to hug Carol.

'It'll be all right, Carol,' he said. 'Whatever it is, we're all here for you, remember that.'

* * *

206

The bungalow was empty at last and the balloons, lights and streamers Lexi had hung up seemed to mock Carol. All that wonderful food gone to waste.

'Why did you do that, Tom?' Carol said tearfully. 'Are you feeling ill?'

'Sick to my stomach,' he murmured. 'I'm so sorry, Carol. I've let you down. I've let everyone down. Even her.'

He looked at Poppy who was sitting beside Carol, leaning against her legs as she sensed she needed comfort.

'I don't think we can keep her, Carol.'

'What? No! She's not going back. She's already lost one owner, she's not going to lose us too.'

'Was it something to do with those guys that came to the door?' Paul asked and Tom's head dropped.

'They came to repossess the car,' he said. 'It's the tip of a very big iceberg. I'm behind with the mortgage and up to my limit on the credit card and they won't raise it any higher. I don't know how it happened, how it all spiralled out of control after a lifetime of being careful and

207

never having any debts. I'm so ashamed and I'm so, so sorry, Carol. I've ruined everything.'

Carol sighed and leaned across the table, covering his hand with her own.

'You're not behind with the mortgage, Tom,' she said.

'I am, love.'

'You're not. We are. We both got carried away buying this place and getting a new car. We just didn't think about the future, about having to retire and losing our income. I'm just as guilty as you.

'I thought we could amble on for ever, but the owners saw what we didn't, that we just couldn't cope. I knew things were tight, but I didn't realise we were in real trouble.'

'Ah, Dad,' Paul said. 'Why didn't you say something sooner? I could have helped. I still can.'

'I am not borrowing money from my son,' Tom said firmly and he was almost quivering at the mere thought of it.

'You don't have to,' Paul said. 'What if I bought the bungalow from you?'

208

Carol forgot for a moment what an awful situation they were in and her face lit up.

'You and Ruth are moving back here?'

Paul's breath whistled through his teeth.

'I'm sorry, Mum. No. Not both of us. I'm sorry to heap more bad news on you just now, but Ruth and I have split up.'

'No!' Carol said. 'I don't believe it. You'll get over it, surely. You'll patch up your differences and get back together.'

'No, Mum. It really is over. It's amicable, we're still friends, we're just not in love with each other any more and we agreed to make the break while we're both still young enough to start again. It's been coming on for a long time.'

'That's so sad,' Tom said. 'I'm so sorry, son. It puts our problems in the shade.'

'We're in the process of selling our house and I was looking for somewhere else to live and as I work for myself, I'm not tied to any particular area. The city no longer holds the attraction it once did.'

'But where will we go?' Carol said. 'Where will we live if you move in here?'

Paul laughed and got up to hug his mother.

'You daft old thing,' he said affectionately. 'You'll live here of course — if you can bear living with me again after all these years.'

'Oh, well . . . ' Carol said. She didn't know how to feel. 'I suppose this gets all of the awful news out of the way in one go. But I don't know if living together would work, Paul. We're all used to doing things our own way.'

'There's only one way to find out, isn't there?' he said. 'If it doesn't work out, we can think again, but this would be a solution in the short term. We need to speak to your bank as soon as possible.'

Tom stood up.

'I'm going to bed,' he said. 'I'll clear up in the morning.'

'Think about what I said, Dad,' Paul said.

'I don't have to,' Tom said. 'We're not selling the bungalow to you or living with you. I got us into this mess and I'll get us out of it. It's a kind offer, but you've done it on the spur of the moment without thinking it through yourself.'

Carol's heart sank. Paul had offered them such a perfect solution and Tom had thrown it back at him.

'I'll talk to him tomorrow,' she said. 'But I don't hold out much hope of changing his mind. His pride is all he has left.'

'And you, Mum,' Paul said. 'And me and all the family and all your friends, too. Neither of you are alone in this.'

Change of Heart

'I'm so worried about Carol and Tom,' Lexi said as Noah dropped them off outside The Beach Hut. 'Do you think they'll be OK?'

'Paul is there,' Noah said. 'He's the eldest and most responsible of their sons. He'll make sure they're all right and I'll pop over to see them on Monday.'

'I wonder what happened,' Beth said. 'One minute Tom was laughing and joking with everyone, cooking food on the barbecue and the next, well . . . ' She shook her head, baffled.

'Someone came to the door to see him,' Noah recalled. 'Perhaps it had something to do with that.'

'He has been acting a bit strangely,' Lexi said. 'Secretive phone calls and hiding the mail.'

'Well, let's not speculate,' Beth said. 'Thanks for the lift, Noah.'

'You're welcome.'

'Noah,' Lexi said, 'I'm really sorry

about being in your house. I honestly didn't damage anything. It was like that when I went there with my. . . with the others. I was shocked when I saw it, to be honest, but I thought it had been abandoned.'

'It had,' Noah said. 'It should never have been left neglected all those years.'

'Doesn't matter,' Beth said. 'Neglected or not, they had no right to damage someone else's property.'

'It's been done over a period of years,' Noah said, 'judging by the graffiti.'

'They said they'd been using the house for a while,' Lexi said. 'To be honest, I thought they were a bit old to still be doing it, but I needed somewhere to stay and lick my wounds.

'I'm sorry, Beth. I've been such an idiot. But I have written down their names. You could speak to their parents before they end up doing something really stupid.'

She held out a piece of paper.

'Are you sure about this, Lexi?' Noah said.

'I'm sure. They're not bad people and

I'd hate them to end up in real trouble. The boat belongs to Josh's dad. He was taking it without permission. That could be dangerous, too.'

'OK.' Noah nodded and pushed the paper in his pocket. 'Thanks for that, Lexi.'

'You haven't been stupid, Lexi,' Beth said. 'We've both made mistakes, but I hope we can put it behind us. If you really hate living here, I'll start looking for something back home.'

'You'd really do that?'

'Nothing is worth us falling out over,' Beth said. 'Not even a house on the beach don't you agree, Noah?'

He looked thoughtful for a moment.

'There have been too many fallings out and too much bad feeling. If I were you and Lexi was my sister, I'd be out of here like a shot if it meant keeping her.' He followed that with a hasty goodnight, then hurried back to his car.

'Wow, he couldn't wait to get away,' Lexi said. 'I thought you two were getting close.'

'Some things just aren't meant to be,' Beth said hollowly.

'Why not? He seems really nice. Is it because of me? Did I ruin it all?'

'No, of course not,' Beth said. 'I managed to do that all by myself. Anyway, you heard him. He thinks I should leave and maybe he's right. We'll talk more tomorrow. Your room is ready for you, Lexi. I mean, the spare room.'

'Oh, Beth, I'm sorry. You don't have to tread on eggshells around me any more. I think we've done enough talking for a while. Can we just enjoy a day together tomorrow and not think about what happens next?'

'Of course,' Beth said, relieved. She wanted to put off the conversation they had to have about leaving for as long as possible.

* * *

Noah drove along the now cleared road to Laburnum Villa. What a roller-coaster of a day it had been and it had ended

215

with him in no doubt about Beth's feelings for him.

She was ready to leave Furze Point for her sister and rightly so, but it would also mean he'd never see her again. He should have taken the opportunity to tell her how he felt about her, but if he had, then she would have felt torn between him and Lexi and that would be wrong.

He knew he had to let her go.

'She's not yours to let go,' he said out loud.

He drove through the entrance gates and imagined how different this would look in the not too distant future. It would be grand again, warm and welcoming. Flowers would bloom and solar lights would light the way along the drive to the house.

He had never considered living here with anyone else, but now when he thought about it, he could see Beth at his side.

But it was just a dream. Nothing could ever come of it.

On Monday morning, Beth gave Lexi

a lift to Tiny Tails.

'These are the kittens and mother cat that Lexi helped me rescue,' Rachel said as they stood outside a large pen. 'I thought she was feral, but something tells me otherwise. I don't think anyone loved her enough to have her spayed, or if they did, she became lost before that happened.'

Beth looked into the angry green eyes of the tabby cat and sighed.

'She looks so fed up,' she said.

'She is,' Rachel said. 'But she'll come round. She's all hisses and spitting at the moment. Goodness knows how many kittens she's had and what she's been through, but that stops now.

'I'll assess her for a home and have her spayed and we'll find good homes for her babies. If she really can't adapt to domestic life, she'll go and live with Fergus on the farm. He's taken a lot of cats and they all seem to settle well.'

'Fergus is lovely, isn't he?' Beth said.

'He is one of the kindest men I've ever met,' Rachel said matter-of-factly. 'He built all my pens here for nothing and if ever I need anything, he's here like a shot. But right now I'm glad you're both here. I have things I want to discuss with you. Come inside and I'll make coffee.'

They sat round a large pine table in Rachel's cosy kitchen with a variety of cats and dogs sprawled around.

'I'm afraid I'm no longer looking for a dog,' Beth said.

'Oh, what changed your mind?'

'Lexi and I are moving back home,' Beth said and she smiled at her sister, but didn't get the expected smile in return.

'I thought we were going to talk about it,' Lexi said.

Beth shrugged.

'I didn't think there was much left to say. You don't like it here, so we'll move. That's what you want, isn't it?'

Lexi sighed.

'It's what I thought I wanted. I was determined to hate it here no matter what, but having lived here for a while, I've grown to like it. Love it, even.'

Rachel looked from one to the other

of them.

'Well, are you staying or not?' she asked bluntly. 'I need to know.'

'We are,' Lexi said. 'If Beth is happy to.'

'I'm happy to,' Beth said, her throat feeling tight.

'Then this is the thing,' Rachel said. 'I have more work than I can handle with the hydrotherapy, grooming and training. I need to take someone on to take some of the workload and also to help out with the rescue. That someone could be you, Lexi.'

'But I'm not qualified,' Lexi said breathlessly.

'No, but I can give you on-the-job training and you could do some days at college. I think you have the skill there, Lexi. I've seen how you are with animals. You have a rare gift. Did you have many pets as a child?'

'None at all,' Beth said. 'We lived in a flat.'

'Then it truly is a gift she has,' Rachel said. 'Think it over and we'll talk some more about what happens next.'

'I don't have to,' Lexi said. 'I'll do it. I'd love to.'

Beth had never seen Lexi so enthused about anything before.

Rachel laughed.

'Even so, I'll give you a few days to think about it and talk it over with Beth. Now to you, Beth. Are you certain you want to stay here if I give Lexi a job? And will you want to rehome a dog?'

'And a cat,' Beth said, then covered her mouth with her hand as if she couldn't believe she'd said it. 'Goodness, I'm getting carried away. I'll have to check into the conditions of my tenancy.'

'You both have a lot to think about,' Rachel said. 'And talk. That most of all.'

The Perfect Answer

'What now?' Lexi asked as they drove away from Tiny Tails.

'We think. We talk,' Beth said. 'And we pop in to see Carol and Tom. I want to check how they are.'

'So are we staying?'

'I hope so,' Beth said. 'If you're sure that's what you really want.'

'Oh, Beth, I loved helping Rachel when she rescued the cat and her kittens. She does so much else too, checking for chips on strays and finding lost pets. She's amazing.

'I never really knew what I wanted to do, but for the first time in my life, I feel as if I know what I want. I know you'll be disappointed about me giving up university.'

'No.' Beth shook her head. 'I'm not disappointed. I thought it was what you wanted. If you're happy, then I'm happy. That's all that matters to me.'

Carol squeezed Noah's arm. 'Tom's out in the garden,' she said. 'He won't talk to us about what's happened.'

'What exactly is it?' Noah asked and Carol looked at Paul and bit her lip.

'He's run up debts,' Paul explained. 'I've said I'll buy the bungalow and live here with them, but he won't have it. I've seen some of the letters he's been hiding. He's on the verge of losing everything. If the bungalow is repossessed, which looks likely, it could end up being sold at way under market value.'

'You could still buy it,' Noah said, pushing back his feelings of shock. It was unlike Tom to have been so reckless, but then circumstances can change for anyone in the blink of an eye and it wasn't difficult to find yourself completely out of your depth.

'I don't think he'd ever forgive me if I did that,' Paul said.

'Is it all right if I go and talk to him?'

'Yes, go ahead,' Carol said. 'Don't

222

expect him to say anything though. He's gone completely silent on us.'

Noah stepped outside into the chill air and walked down to where Tom was digging a fork into his vegetable patch.

'I don't know why I'm bothering,' he said without looking up. 'We won't be here long enough to harvest anything I plant.'

Noah let out a short laugh.

'I remember sitting on the jetty pulling my crabbing line up for the umpteenth time and complaining because I hadn't caught anything. Remember what you told me?'

'Patience,' Tom said with a smile. 'You didn't give the crabs time to latch on to the bait. But patience won't get me out of this mess, Noah.'

'OK, then remember when we were out on the shore cockle picking? I sank up to my knee in mud and cried. I thought I was going to be buried alive. Remember what you said then?'

This time Tom laughed out loud.

'I shouldn't laugh,' he said. 'You were

so scared, poor little boy. I said there was no hole big enough that we couldn't dig you out of and we set about getting you out. But you could have pulled your leg out yourself if you hadn't been frozen with fear.'

'I lost my trainer,' Noah said. 'The mud took it. So, Tom, you might lose something, but you don't have to lose everything. I'll never forget how I felt when you, Rob and Fergus all started to dig. I felt so surrounded by love and although my pride took a bit of a battering, I was fine.'

'You were a kid.'

'A human being, as are you. Let Paul help you if he wants to. Anyway, I'm not here to talk about you. As you once said to me, you're not the only person in the world, you know.'

'I said that?' Tom said, running his hand through his white hair.

'I'm going to restore Laburnum Villa and I've got big plans for it. I'm going to take on a massage therapist, acupuncturist, maybe even a hypnotherapist.'

'Pfft!' Tom scoffed. 'Hokum.'

'Not at all. I've benefited from all that and I want others to do the same in the peaceful atmosphere of my grandmother's mansion. I'm going to do up the stables too and offer riding lessons.

'I've looked into it, Tom, done my research and Furze Point is lacking in all those things. The thing is, I'll need staff. I'll need a Tom to do all those things that Toms do and a Carol to make people feel welcome and comfortable, which is what Carols do best.'

'We're too old.'

'I'm not asking you to climb all over beach houses in all weathers repairing roofs and fighting with dodgy generators. It'll be the lightest of property maintenance and managing the cleaning staff with a bit of admin thrown in.'

'Well, it's good of you to think of us, Noah boy,' Tom said. 'But I don't honestly know what's to become of us once we lose this place. We'll be homeless.'

'Didn't I say?' Noah said. 'Remember

225

Corky's Cottage?'

Tom nodded slowly. Corky's Cottage was a small one-storey building a short distance from Laburnum Villa. Corky had worked for Freda's father and then for her up until his death. Noah could barely remember him, but he remembered the cottage.

'It hasn't been vandalised by the elements or people. It needs a bit of work, but it won't take much to make it habitable. It's yours if you want it. Comes with the job.'

Tom's eyes reddened for a moment. He looked like a man who'd cried so much, there were no tears left to fall.

'And in case you're wondering, I'd always planned to ask you,' Noah said. 'You and Carol were like a mum and dad to me. It might have been a long time ago, but I've never forgotten your kindness.'

'What does your dad say about it?'

'He's pretty furious,' Noah said with a grin. 'We had a long talk about it and he's accepted that this is what I'm going

226

to do. There was no way I would ever in a million years build a housing estate on that land.'

Tom turned to look at the house where Carol and Paul were standing side by side in the conservatory.

'We've got jobs,' he shouted. 'And somewhere to live!'

The back door flew open and Carol burst out.

'Did you just say what I think you said?'

'We can sell this place. Remember Corky's Cottage?'

'Do I!' Carol said. 'It was that lovely little cottage that made me hanker after a bungalow all these years.'

'Noah says it's ours. We have to work, though. Are you going to be all right doing that? Working up at Scott's Mansion?'

Carol clapped her hands.

'I never wanted to retire,' she said. 'It sounds perfect.'

'And you may well benefit from some of the therapists who will have rooms in the house,' Noah said. 'We'll have you running up and down the hill again in no time.'

There was such laughter, that Poppy ran round the garden in a rare display of excitement.

'I'd still like to buy the bungalow,' Paul said. 'Will you let me do that now?'

'We'd like nothing better than for you to have it,' Tom said. 'Would we, girl?'

Carol laughed. They'd come through this, perhaps with a little money from the sale of the bungalow, their debts repaid, their pride intact.

Where the Heart Is

'Is Tom all right?' Beth asked as Carol opened the door to let her in. She could already feel the atmosphere had changed. That air of something being terribly wrong had lifted, or was it Carol's smile that told her that something exciting was happening?

'He's more than all right,' Carol said. 'See for yourself.'

'Ah, Beth, Lexi!' Tom burst into the hall. 'We're going to have our party tonight. Most of the food is OK and it seems such a pity to waste it. Paul put as much as he could in the fridge. We have so much to celebrate. Life is good!'

Beth and Lexi laughed. What a change. On Saturday he'd seemed so despairing.

'It is all right to have a party on a Monday night, isn't it?' Carol asked uncertainly. 'I mean people have work and school . . . '

'It's just one night,' Beth said. 'I'm sure everyone will be fine with that.'

'And all is well with you girls?' Carol said and the sisters looked at each other and smiled.

'Couldn't be better,' Beth said and she put her arm round Lexi. 'We're staying in Furze Point. Lexi's going to work for Rachel and I'm going to get a dog and or a cat, if I'm allowed.'

'Why shouldn't you be?' Tom said. 'There are no stipulations about pets, within reason of course.'

'Noah's going to open a complementary health centre at Laburnum Villa,' Carol explained. 'He wants Tom and I to work for him. He thinks it'll be in great demand, not just from the locals, but from the summer visitors, too. He's a qualified chiropractor.'

'No,' Beth said, her stomach sinking. 'He's a civil engineer. He told me.'

'Yes, yes he was,' Tom said, 'because that was his father's business and he was channelled into it so to speak, but he realised he wanted to do his own thing. It's only recently that everything has finally fallen into place.'

'And your dog walking and pet sitting business?' Beth asked.

'Is up and running and I'll honour my current commitments,' Tom said. 'But maybe someone else would like to take it on. Another string to her ever-growing bow?' He looked at Lexi.

'It's an idea,' she said. 'I'll run it past Rachel tonight at the party.'

'Will you stay, Lexi? Help me get all the lights back up? Tom and Paul have an appointment at the bank and there's so much to do.'

Lexi looked at Beth.

'Good idea,' she said. 'But I have to get back to the Beach Hut. I'm expecting a delivery. I will be back this evening, though. Would you like me to bring you something to change into when I come back, Lexi?'

'My black top with the silver studs and black jeans, please,' Lexi said. 'And some make-up. You know what I need.'

'Yes,' Beth said, pleased beyond reason that things were normal between them again. 'Yes, I do.'

★ ★ ★

Noah paced up and down outside the Beach Hut. Beth and Lexi appeared to have gone already. He couldn't believe they would have left without saying goodbye.

There was something about Beth that reminded him of his grandmother. He could imagine her storming up and down the beach house steps if she thought someone had been up to no good.

But they were very different in other ways. Gran was a hoarder who hung on to things that meant a lot to her whereas Beth had managed to pack her whole life into a car.

The rumble of an engine made him stop pacing and step to the side of the road just as Beth's car came round the bend. She opened her window as she passed.

'I'm going to park in the car park,' she called out. 'I'm expecting a delivery and I don't want to get in the way of the lorry.'

He watched her walk back from the car park, still walking awkwardly.

'So, you're a chiropractor,' she said.

'You've been to see Carol and Tom?' he said with a rueful smile.

'Why keep it secret?'

'I don't know. I thought if I told anyone what I planned that it would all fall through, but that's not going to happen, Beth. I'm going to do it and I'm going to make a success of it.'

'But why? Why give up a perfectly good career as a civil engineer and take up something that could hardly be more different?'

'I had an accident on a site,' he said. 'Pretty bad. I was living on painkillers and in a constant state of misery when a friend suggested I see a chiropractor. I know some people dismiss it, but it was like a miracle.

'When I first saw Leonard, he promised to have me off painkillers in six weeks and in the end he did it in five. I just thought I wanted to be able to help people like that and so I retrained.'

'It sounds wonderful,' Beth said.

'I could help you recover from your fall,' he said.

'Really?'

'I can't make it better, but I can help speed your recovery.'

'I'll think about it,' she said. 'Thank you for offering.'

'Unless you're leaving . . . ' he said. He'd meant to build up to the subject gradually, not just blurt it out like that.

'Do you want us to?'

'What? No! I mean, it has nothing to do with me. But you shouldn't stay here unless you really want to, both of you.'

'We're staying,' she said with a smile. 'Lexi's got a plan for her future and a job and I . . . ' She shoved her hands in her pockets and looked out at the sea. It was rough today, the waves topped with foam.

Gulls skimmed the surface and dark clouds bubbled up on the horizon. The wind coming off the sea was cold. Behind them, the trees rustled.

'I love it here. It's the most beautiful

place on earth.'

He came to stand at her side and looked out at the sea too.

'Wonderful, isn't it? I used to love it here in winter. It was so different. Gran and I always had a walk along the beach on Christmas Day. I always spent Christmas here.'

'With your parents?'

He laughed.

'No.'

'I can't imagine not spending Christmas with my parents. It wasn't the same after Dad died, but Mum did her best, then we lost Mum, too, but we still have our memories.'

'And I have mine,' he said. 'It's the way of life isn't it? You wouldn't appreciate the happy memories if you didn't have sad ones.'

'That's one way of looking at it.' She smiled. 'Anyway, were you waiting for me?'

'Yes, I . . . ' He hesitated. 'I drove over to Stoursley today and looked up those names Lexi gave me. I don't think we'll be troubled by them again. They're not bad kids and their parents are going to talk to them. Josh's father wasn't very happy when he found out they'd been using his boat.'

'That's good,' Beth said. 'Was there anything else?'

He was about to answer when the lorry trundled up.

Beth's heart was pumping like a mad thing as she saw the delivery in. It was just a small one. She didn't need much stock for the coming months. She half expected Noah to leave, but he stayed right where he was. Every time she looked over at him, her heart jumped to see he was watching her.

She signed for the delivery and told the driver that he could turn round by the car park.

'Never been here before,' he said. 'I thought when I came down the road and saw the sea at the end that my sat nav was messing me about.'

'It's an unusual place,' she said.

'You can say that again.'

'Would you like a cup of tea or anything before you go?' She asked, but hoped he'd say no because she wanted to talk to Noah.

'Very kind of you, but I'd best be getting on. See you again.'

She hurried over to join Noah on the beach. Rain had started to fall. It was sharp and stinging.

'Carol and Tom are having their party tonight,' she said. 'Will you go?'

'Definitely. I can pick you and Lexi up if you like.'

'She's already there. I have to take her a change of clothes. But a lift would be lovely, thank you. You were about to tell me what you were doing here when the delivery arrived.'

He looked down at her for a long time and she thought she'd melt in the warmth of his eyes despite being buffeted by the wind, rain and the spray from the sea.

'I thought you'd gone already,' he said. 'I thought I'd never see you again.'

'I wouldn't have gone without saying goodbye,' she said. 'And I would have waited until they found a replacement.'

'We hardly know each other and yet I feel as if I've known you all my life. You probably know more about me than anyone else on earth and when I'm with you, I feel happy and at peace.

'I'm sorry. Forget I said anything. That all sounds so cheesy. I don't want this to ruin our friendship. I just don't want you to go away, Beth.'

He turned to walk away and she reached out and grabbed his sleeve.

'Don't go,' she said.

The squall had well and truly arrived now. Their hair was wet, plastered to their heads and rain poured off their chins and noses.

'We should go inside,' she said and they hurried over to the Beach Hut and Beth closed the door behind them.

They stood dripping all over the floor, faces red from the wind.

Noah put his hands on Beth's shoulders.

'Beth, what I said . . .'

'Don't you dare say you're sorry,' she

said. 'Did you mean it?'

'Every word.'

'I've always said that actions speak louder than words,' she said. 'Lexi got fed up hearing it.'

He was so strong and capable, but right now he looked bewildered and confused as only a man in love can. Not that Beth knew anything about love, not until now. There was only one thing left to do.

'Kiss me, Noah,' she said.

He smiled uncertainly, then realised she was serious and pulled her into his arms. Beth realised she'd been longing for this from the moment he'd rescued her on the road and it was every bit as wonderful as she'd hoped.

'Wow,' he whispered. 'I was right, Beth. I've never felt like this about anyone before.'

'Neither have I,' she said honestly. 'Noah, from the moment I first saw you, I knew you were special. Do you believe in love at first sight?'

'I didn't,' he laughed softly. 'Until I met you. I don't think I would have come back here if I wasn't so desperate to see you again.' He pulled her into his arms again. 'I love you. Do you love me, Beth?'

She hugged him tighter.

'Yes,' she said. 'I do love you. With all my heart. But we have to get ready for the party.'

'Ah, yes, the party,' he said reluctantly. 'Is it awful to say I'd rather stay here with you?'

She laughed, pushing him away playfully.

'Yes, it is,' she said. 'Go and change into some dry clothes and I'll see you soon.'

* * *

There were even more people at Carol and Tom's bungalow for this party. More food had been brought and when Noah and Beth walked in, Lexi grabbed the bag with her clothes and hurried off to get changed.

She'd just come back when Tom

tapped his wine glass with a spoon until he had the attention of everyone.

'There's just something I'd like to say,' he said and he turned to Beth, Lexi and Noah. 'Welcome home.'

A cheer went up.

'Thank you!' Lexi shouted, laughing. 'It's great to be here.'

Noah looked round at all the familiar, happy faces from his past.

'I can't tell you how much it means to be back home with my family again. Thank you all.'

'Oh, mate!' Fergus said and Beth quickly handed him a napkin to dab at his eyes.

'Thank you for making us so welcome,' Beth said and once again, she was hugging everyone. Coming here had been the best decision of her life and looking at Lexi, happily chatting to Rachel, she knew they'd really found home.